The Mystery of the Ruby Queens

The CONNIE BLAIR *Mystery Stories*

BY BETSY ALLEN

THE CLUE IN BLUE

THE RIDDLE IN RED

PUZZLE IN PURPLE

THE SECRET OF BLACK CAT GULCH

THE GREEN ISLAND MYSTERY

THE GHOST WORE WHITE

THE YELLOW WARNING

THE GRAY MENACE

THE BROWN SATCHEL MYSTERY

PERIL IN PINK

THE SILVER SECRET

THE MYSTERY OF THE RUBY QUEENS

She was completely obscured from the intruder's view

A CONNIE BLAIR MYSTERY

The Mystery of the Ruby Queens

By

BETSY ALLEN

Grosset & Dunlap

PUBLISHERS   NEW YORK

Contents

CHAPTER 1

Visitor to Fifth Street

"I HAVE my lunch this time, Aunt Bet!"

Connie Blair held up a package wrapped in brown paper and tied with a string. For the past week she had been carrying her lunch to work. To save time in the morning, she made the sandwiches the night before, but twice she had left them in the refrigerator where she had put them to keep them fresh.

"Now all you need, dear, is a union card." Elizabeth Easton smiled as she poured herself a second cup of coffee from the percolator on the dinette table. Dressed for her job as stylist at Campion's, one of Philadelphia's most exclusive shops, she was smart and businesslike in a dark suit and a string of tiny, cream-colored pearls.

Connie eyed the pearls, which were the color

of her own clear skin, and glanced with admiration at her aunt's nylon-clad legs and trim suède pumps. Then she looked down at the loafers and socks she was wearing, and frowned at the faded blue jeans that covered her slim legs below the hem of her tweed coat.

No one, seeing her in this garb, would suspect that she, too, was a young woman with a very respectable position at the well-known Reid and Renshaw Advertising Agency. She felt exactly like a day laborer. But, although Connie didn't know it, the perfection of her smoothly combed blond hair gave the impression that she was modeling casual sportswear for a specialty shop.

"I'm not going on the bus again in this getup!" she announced, her brown eyes filled with sudden decision. "This morning, I'll walk!"

"It's bitter cold out, and it's more than ten blocks," her aunt warned.

"I know. But seventeen-year-old girls just don't run around a big city in *jeans*. I mean, nice ones don't. People stare at me on the bus, Aunt Bet. I know they disapprove."

"Maybe you could pin a sign on yourself explaining—'I'm on a special assignment . . . I'm doing research work in a dirty old building and—'"

"Will do"—Connie interrupted, laughing, as she opened the door of the apartment—"tomorrow. But if I'm going to walk, I'd better start. See you at dinner."

Living with Aunt Bet was fun. Although she

was Connie's mother's sister, Aunt Bet didn't seem middle-aged; certainly not thirty-seven. And Connie was eternally grateful for the suggestion that she share the apartment. Otherwise, Connie's family probably would not have let her take a job away from home.

The first few blocks of the walk weren't uncomfortable, but as Connie cut diagonally across Independence Square, the early December wind was biting and cruel. Clutching the turned-up collar of her coat with one hand to protect her ears, she tried, with the other, to hold her coat from whipping away from her legs. The package of lunch helped, acting as an anchor, but she began to shiver and think longingly of the warmth of her father's hardware store in the small town of Meadowbrook. Mr. Blair "opened up" early. She could see him now, already waiting on customers, advising them on their problems. She could visualize her twin sister Kit, too, making up orders, answering the telephone. She could almost smell the distinctive odor of new wire screening mingled with that of tanned leather.

The clock in the tower of Independence Hall was just nearing eight-thirty. About now, at home, her mother would be saying good-by to Toby, her ten-year-old brother, as he started off for school. Toby wouldn't be cold. Although Meadowbrook was only a two-hour train ride from Philadelphia, the air there was crisp, dry, bracing. It was the dampness rising from the river that made it so bitter here.

For a moment a wave of homesickness swept over Connie. Then she passed a policeman patrolling the Square. She had seen him several times before and he smiled at her and wished her good morning.

Instantly Connie felt better and was once more her well-adjusted self. She missed her family, especially Kit, but not for anything would she have traded her life in the glamorous world of advertising.

The intriguing thing was that it was so ever-changing. For instance, who'd have imagined two weeks ago that instead of being behind a desk in the offices of Reid and Renshaw, she'd be working downtown in the heart of Independence Mall and Independence National Park.

The area fascinated Connie. It was the Revolutionary part of the city now being rehabilitated as a joint municipal, state, and federal project. The Mall was being cleared northward to the Benjamin Franklin Bridge approach which crossed the Delaware River to New Jersey. The Park eventually would be cleared from Independence Square eastward to the river.

Many of the old buildings and homes had suffered unfortunate alterations since Colonial times. Now these were being remodeled into office buildings and commercial establishments with authentic Colonial fronts. All unsightly structures were being razed. Those historic buildings that were intact were simply getting a face lifting.

What could be more exciting than to walk upon

the same bricks that George Washington and
Thomas Jefferson had walked? Or to glance, whenever you pleased, at the stately hall where the
Declaration of Independence had been signed
. . . or at the steps from which it had been read
to the assembled populace. Connie was delighted
that Mr. Renshaw had given her a chance to be
part of such an important project.

"Sansom Paint and Paper Company," the tall,
handsome member of the firm had told her, re-
ferring to a Reid and Renshaw client of long
standing, "have permission to research the wallpaper in the old Calder mansion—the one that's
being done over for an insurance company office.
Sansom intends bringing out a new line of Colonial prints and paints which they want to be
authentic. Georgia Cameron did a similar job on
the Williamsburg restoration."

"I know," Connie commented. "It sounded
terribly exciting."

She and Georgia had discussed it at odd mo-
ments during their business trip to Bermuda
where Connie had solved *The Green Island Mystery* and Georgia had met Philip Tremont whom
she later married.

"Well"—Mr. Renshaw smiled—"with your art
school training you should be able to handle this
job easily. It's merely a matter of copying the wallpaper for design and color as the crew peel it off
layer after layer."

"It sounds like fun," Connie replied, and it had
been—every minute of it—so far. Just seeing the

patterns of the papers—which had been applied so long ago was like finding buried treasure.

She liked all the people with whom she was working, especially Happy Wallace, an architectural student from the University of Pennsylvania, employed on a part-time basis by the company that was doing the remodeling. Her closest associate on the job was the photographer, Lance Hurley. Lance was documenting the entire house, so that the interior views might be used in the Sansom Company's advertising brochure to introduce the new line to the trade.

Connie crossed Fifth Street and looked up at the Calder mansion. Even in its semineglected state it bore all the symmetrical dignity of eighteenth-century Georgian architecture. It followed the graceful elegant style of the renowned Christopher Wren, who had designed so many London buildings and palaces in the middle seventeen hundreds. The paneled double doors were topped by an exquisitely delicate fanlight and flanked by beautifully proportioned small-paned windows.

The red brick had taken on the gentleness of time. Three stories up, the gray slate roof complemented the mellowed brick.

Entering through the unlocked door, Connie took off her coat and laid it on a pile of others in the hall.

"Hi, Lance," she greeted the photographer. "How did yesterday's shots come out?"

"So-so," Lance replied. "I've got to get my Graflex overhauled. It's developed a light leak in the bellows. I'll try the Leica today, even if it means enlargements."

Connie glanced at the 35-mm. German camera slung across Lance Hurley's thin shoulders. Lance was tall, about twenty years old, Connie judged, and he would have been attractive if he paid more attention to his personal appearance. Granted everyone was wearing old clothes on Fifth Street, but Lance's were particularly sloppy and there was no excuse for his hair which had been sorely in need of a barber's clippers for days.

Until last week, Connie had not met, nor heard of, Lance. To her knowledge, the art director at Reid and Renshaw had never commissioned him to do a job for the agency before. Quite likely he was a new "find." Certainly he seemed to be a capable photographer and Connie liked him. Although he was quiet and not given to small talk, he was friendly and it had been at his suggestion that they had dispensed with the formal "Miss" and "Mr." in favor of more casual names. Occasionally Lance became so engrossed in his work, or in his own thoughts, that he failed to answer when spoken to—or, at best, mumbled some inarticulate reply which gave the impression that he was sullen. But Connie was quite accustomed by now to what she termed his moods, and put them down to artistic temperament.

"Has Happy come in yet?" she asked.

"No. He said he had classes this morning. He'll be down after lunch, I guess."

Connie remembered that Happy Wallace's

hours were indefinite to say the least. It must have been because of his remarkable knowledge of Early American buildings that the construction company permitted him to do their surveying work on this haphazard time basis.

But Connie had the feeling, too, that Happy was being groomed for a permanent place with the company after his graduation. Young architects with his knowledge and ability weren't easily acquired in this technical age.

Pushing her hair back from her face, Connie unpacked her art materials and started sketching and recording the layer of wallpaper now exposed in one corner. (Peeling off the papers was an exacting process and the workmen limited themselves to a small area at a time.) Connie had only a small patch to work from, about a foot square. But it was an exciting patch, a pretty pattern of red cherries on a white background, the first of the Colonial prints to show beneath more recent layers here in the hall. The rest of the wall was still covered in dull tan, the choice of Miss Carrie Calder who had been the last person to live in the house. She had died a few months ago, in July, at the age of seventy-nine.

"Think how old that cherry print is!" Connie exclaimed. "And it may be hiding an even older one. Oh, Lance, aren't you just dying to see?"

But Lance didn't answer. He was eying a stepladder near the door, figuring a new angle for his next shot.

Connie ripped off a sheet of tracing paper and

started to outline the pattern. Later she would make two transfers to her water-color sketch block. On one, she would faithfully reproduce the colors as she saw them. On the other, she would try to visualize the more intense original hues that had existed before time, humidity, paste, and plaster dust had dimmed them. Between the two, the manufacturer would find a practical compromise for the final printing.

She was tracing with bold strokes, stepping aside occasionally to let Lance get a flash-bulb shot of the wainscoting. The crew had moved upstairs and were hammering in the rear bedrooms that were being remodeled for the executive suite. She and Lance were alone in the hall.

Except for the bench, which everyone used as a coat rack, and a few old kitchen chairs and the stepladder, the house was devoid of furnishings. The hall, flanked on one side by a large drawing room and on the other by a paneled dining room, was the center of activity with workmen coming and going, shouldering long lengths of boards, lugging kegs of nails and other appurtenances of carpentry. A curved stairway rose directly opposite the front doorway, just back of the arches leading to the side rooms. It was a gracious and spacious entrance. It ran the full depth of the house, giving access to the rear garden.

Connie never felt its present bareness. In her subconscious mind she always pictured it immaculate, with a tall clock in the corner, a lowboy along one wall, delicate Sheraton chairs at the side and a colorful Aubusson rug covering the waxed random-width floor boards.

"How about climbing up on that," Lance said, indicating the stepladder, "for an action take. *Work in Progress* or some such thing."

With her pencil and paper in hand, Connie postured on the top of the ladder as Lance had instructed, pretending to draw from an imaginary spot high on the wall. But Lance wasn't satisfied with the result. "I've got to do it over. I think the exposure was wrong that time."

While he fiddled with the camera aperture, Connie glanced at the door. "Kit would adore these old locks. It's part of the hardware business in her blood. Would you have an extra print of them, Lance . . . for me to send her?"

"I can dig one up, I guess," Lance told her. "I'll try to remember to bring it along tomorrow."

"Thanks, Lance. I'd appreciate that." Connie resumed her pose. "It's lucky for the Sansom company these walls were never scraped. Incidentally, why weren't they? The place has been in the Calder family almost two hundred years."

Actually she wouldn't have been surprised if Lance, preoccupied now with his camera for the retake shot, had not answered, but the vehemence of his response was so startling that she almost lost her footing on the ladder.

"I can't tell you about the early Calders. But Carrie was too mean to do anything except by the cheapest route. And that probably didn't include scraping!"

"Why, Lance, how can you say she was mean? I mean, did you know her?"

"Yes, but I rarely saw her," he said curtly. "And if you want any more information about the house—why it was scraped or why it wasn't— ask Montgomery Calder. He owns it."

The finality of his tone ended their brief conversation. He flashed another bulb, and then, without a word, gathered up his equipment and disappeared into the dining room.

Connie got off the ladder and resumed her work of tracing the pattern on her sketch block. Lance's attitude concerning Miss Calder interested her. He had sounded as though he had an active enmity against the old lady and yet he had admitted he had rarely seen her. Was it possible that his artistic sense was so incensed by the neglect of a fine residence that he had thought himself into an imagined dislike of Miss Calder?

Although she was a notably wealthy woman, she had been somewhat of a recluse. And certainly, the deplorable condition of the house was evidence that she had spent little money on repairs during the forty years in which she had lived there.

Although Connie couldn't share Lance's dislike for someone with whom she had never been acquainted, she had to agree that the poor quality of the dull tan paper attested to the fact, as Lance had pointed out, that Miss Calder had done things "by the cheapest route."

At home, her mother always insisted that the walls be scraped before repapering because the net result was a better job. Even if Miss Calder hadn't wanted to go to the extra expense, it was odd that in all the years, a former owner hadn't had it done.

A cold draft hit her suddenly between the shoulders. Turning, she saw Montgomery Calder enter the hallway. Tall and erect, a slightly graying man in his fifties, he was, to Connie, the essence of a "perfect gentleman." Immaculately groomed, he had a charm that made even the most insignificant workman on the job feel at ease with "the boss." For, as president of the insurance company for which the building was being remodeled, he *was* the boss. After he had inherited the house from his aunt, Caroline Calder, he had decided to become part of the Restoration and move his offices from their present uptown location to the Square.

Normally, when he came in, he chatted a minute or two with Connie, but this morning he merely threw his hat on the bench, and without bothering to take off his overcoat, started upstairs to inspect the progress on the executive offices.

Halfway up, he paused. "Miss Blair . . ."

"Yes, Mr. Calder."

"I'm expecting a visitor. Or, I should say, I may have a visitor," he amended, sighing. "Since you'll be here in the hall, will you call me if I do?"

"Of course, Mr. Calder," Connie promised.

Only yesterday, Mr. Calder had told her that he had instructed his secretary not to disturb him for business reasons while he was at the new building on Fifth Street. "Nothing's so important that it can't wait until I get back to my desk," Connie remembered he had said. So, whoever he was expecting must be coming to see him on a different matter—a matter, which, to judge from his sigh and the worried expression on his face, he would rather have avoided.

Just as Connie was about to resume tracing the pattern, the doorbell rang with such insistence that it startled her, and the pencil fell from her hand.

Connie retrieved it and, getting up, went to answer the bell. Undoubtedly it was Mr. Calder's visitor, because anyone connected with the remodeling project simply walked in. As she passed the sidelight window to the left of the double door, she noticed a station wagon parked at the curb. It was so long it looked like a bus. In the front seat, sitting bolt upright, was a large brown-and-white English setter. Connie could not see who was on the front step of the house, but the dog's head was turned and his gaze was riveted in that direction.

CHAPTER 2

Furor Over a Fire

"Is Montgomery Calder here?" The question was curt.

Momentarily, Connie was taken aback. "He's—he's on the second floor," she faltered, instinctively moving a little away from the tall, angular, and rather homely woman standing outside the door.

"I want to talk to him," the woman announced, pushing past Connie and on into the hall. She was wearing a full-length mink coat that Connie could tell at a glance was of the finest quality, and a pair of mud-caked laced boots. A green woolen cap with a tassel partly covered her dark hair.

"I'll call him," Connie offered, recovering her composure. "If you care to sit down, there's a chair in the living room."

14

The woman ignored Connie's mention of the chair. "Don't bother calling him. I'll find him myself." She started up the stairs, and then, midway, turned and smiled back at Connie. "Thank you," she said graciously, as though suddenly she had remembered her manners.

"She's upset," Connie decided sympathetically. "That's why she seemed so overbearing at first." Her smile certainly had been sweet. She was about forty, Connie judged, and from the appearance of her boots and the presence of the dog in the station wagon, she had evidently driven into town from the country or the suburbs. But how she was going to discuss anything with Mr. Calder upstairs, Connie couldn't imagine. The din of the hammering up there was deafening!

Picking up her sketch pad, Connie pulled the stepladder closer to the wall. Her feet were tired from standing and there was no reason why she shouldn't sit down to work. A second later she heard Mr. Calder's voice on the landing several feet above her head.

"Come out here, Maryanne," he said. "The noise isn't as bad."

Connie didn't intend to eavesdrop, but the stair well acted as a sound chute and she couldn't help overhearing Mr. Calder's part of an obvious argument.

"Of course they were willed to you, Maryanne! No one is disputing that fact . . . of course you could have them, but they aren't here!"

There was a moment's silence, then Mr. Calder

spoke again, his voice a little testy. "Oh, come now, my dear. Drake has fine-tooth-combed the entire house—"

Connie tried to concentrate on her work to the exclusion of listening to a discussion that was none of her business, but the woman named Maryanne clomped down the stairs in her heavy boots and continued the argument not three feet from her.

"I never did get anywhere with you, Montgomery! And I still insist *she did not give them away*. She promised them to me when I was a child. She even let me hold one occasionally. I knew their names and their histories . . ."

Before Mr. Calder could answer, Maryanne crossed the hall angrily, and without bothering to close the front door, rushed out to the station wagon. Connie saw her throw her arms around the setter and bury her head against his shoulder as though she were terribly depressed.

Mr. Calder had followed her downstairs. He closed the door and turned to Connie. "Miss Blair," he said distractedly, "if you see six queens running around here anywhere, grab them."

"Six queens?" she repeated.

"Yes. They're figurines. Sèvres porcelain. Rarer than Meissen, I think. Anyway, Aunt Carrie—the Miss Calder who used to live here"— he explained, "willed them to my cousin Maryanne Jessup. But they've disappeared."

"Were they stolen?" Connie's question was a natural response to his statement.

Mr. Calder shook his head and smiled wanly. "No. Aunt Carrie simply gave them away, apparently. She did a lot of queer things before she died . . . caused quite a furor. But that's a family detail. You wouldn't be interested.

"Or would you?" he asked suddenly. "Come to think of it, when Renshaw told me you would be working here on the Sansom project, he also mentioned that you were quite a sleuth. In fact, Miss Blair, he was very complimentary. Said you had solved some mighty baffling mysteries. Is that true?"

To have agreed would have sounded like boasting. "I—I was fortunate, I guess," Connie countered, "in finding the answers."

"Well, if you could find the answer to the puzzle of the missing figurines, I'd be eternally grateful!" Mr. Calder exclaimed with real sincerity. "Understand," he amended, "I honestly don't think there *is* any mystery, or puzzle, connected with them, but if they *are* around here, and if you could locate them, well . . . Want to hear the circumstances?"

Connie nodded. "I'd be happy to, Mr. Calder."

"It's like this," he began, sitting down on the first step. "Aunt Carrie willed jewelry and gewgaws to one member of the family and then gave them to another shortly before she died, without telling about the bequest." The ironic little smile had faded and his face showed definite strain, as though he had been worrying over the situation. "For instance, she left one nephew her silver coffee service, a magnificent set, and then gave it to another nephew without telling a soul. It caused bad feeling between their wives, as you can understand . . ."

Connie nodded. She could very well understand. It was the sort of happening that could split a family apart. But she said nothing and let Mr. Calder continue. He acted like a man who was getting a weight off his mind.

"We always had been so close. But now half the family isn't speaking to the other half. And," he added thoughtfully, looking at the floor, "she did it all so slyly. She'd drop someone a note asking the person to come see her . . . always on Thursday when the maid was off for the day. Then she'd present the gift and insist that it not be mentioned until after she died.

"Why she did it, we'll never know. Perhaps she had some quixotic idea that the person she gave them to was more deserving than the person to whom they were bequeathed. Maybe she intended rewriting her will to fit the new concept. But we'll never know."

"But the figurines? No one in the family received *them?*"

"No. I imagine they must have been given to an outsider. In her younger days, Aunt Carrie was quite a traveler. She knew people all over the world. Whoever has them may be in Timbuktu."

In her mind, Connie reviewed Mr. Calder's brief conversation with his cousin Maryanne. Evidently Maryanne did not share his theory that the Queens had been given away. As if thinking aloud, she asked, "What does your cousin think?"

"Maryanne? Oh, she insists Aunt Carrie put them away for her for safekeeping. She's obsessed with some childish drivel about secret hiding places in old houses. It's ridiculous, of course, but Maryanne is convinced they are around the property somewhere." He stopped, as though he had summed up the situation satisfactorily.

But Connie was not satisfied. "May I ask you a question, Mr. Calder?"

"Certainly, Miss Blair. Anything you like."

"If your cousin is right in thinking her aunt wanted her to have the figurines, why didn't Miss Calder give them to her directly?"

"Oh . . . Well, you see, Miss Blair, Maryanne had already left for Europe when Aunt Carrie started this giving-away business. She was in Europe when Aunt Carrie died. We cabled her not to break her trip, which she had been planning for years, to come home for the funeral. After all, there was nothing she could do. Nellie, the housemaid, stayed on here until August and disposed of Aunt Carrie's personal effects. The end of October, we started the remodeling and Maryanne got back to the States about a week later. It was then she learned her inheritance was missing and it was then that I had Drake make a search—"

The door opened with a bang and Happy Wallace literally burst into the hall. "Hi, everybody. It's snowing."

"Hello, Wallace," Mr. Calder greeted, getting

off the step. "Thought you weren't due in until after lunch."

"It is after lunch. Mine, I mean," Happy corrected, brushing the snow from the shoulders of his sheepskin-lined coat. The coat made him seem even taller and huskier than his actual six feet, one-ninety. "I had brunch after my ten-o'clock class."

Ordinarily, Connie would have been delighted to see Happy at any hour of the day. She had known him only a week, but he attracted her more than anyone she had met for a long time. She liked his direct manner of speaking and his merry eyes that so exactly matched the brown of his close-cropped hair.

But why, oh why, hadn't Happy altered his routine of eating two meals in one just this once? If he'd had breakfast and lunch separately, he would have arrived downtown later and not interrupted Mr. Calder's provocative story of the Queens. As it was, with Happy here, Mr. Calder probably would say no more.

He didn't. He glanced at his watch and picked up his hat. "It's five to twelve. I may as well get a bite myself."

"Have a good game," Happy called after him.

"Game?" Connie echoed, when Mr. Calder had gone.

"Yep, game. He goes uptown to the Lincoln Club and bowls at noon. Has chow sent down to the alleys."

Connie smiled reflectively, picturing her father

grabbing his "bite" at the nearest lunch counter. In Meadowbrook there were no exclusive clubs like the Lincoln Club. "Philadelphians have a lovely life," she mused.

"Some do," Happy agreed, without a trace of resentment. " 'But the stars belong to everyone,' " he quoted, grinning his infectious smile. "And so does the lunch hour. Hear ye!"

The noon whistle at one of the mills by the river began its wail. Immediately the noise of hammering and sawing in the rooms above stopped.

"It's time for all good union members to knock off," Happy rambled on. "And you, too, Miss Wallpaper. Did you bring sandwiches?"

"They're on the bench with the coats."

Happy tossed his coat among the others and returned with the brown-paper package. Connie spread it beside her on the ladder.

"Have a hard-boiled egg?"

"I told you, I've eaten."

"Have one, anyway. There are two."

"Thanks," he said, politely taking the smaller egg and pointing it toward the wall. "That cherry print is real purty, ma'am."

"Isn't it? And, Hap, I've been wondering, too, why weren't these walls ever scraped?"

He looked at her quizzically. She had told him about some of her experiences, particularly her most recent one in solving *The Silver Secret,* and Connie sensed that he now wondered what was creeping into her mind.

"Oh, I didn't mean there was any mystery about it. I don't run around dreaming them up. I just think it's odd."

"What's odd?" Happy's glance had strayed from the wall to Connie's shining hair.

"The fact that the walls were never scraped, silly."

"It's not odd, Connie," Happy explained, becoming grave as he did whenever his factual knowledge was called on for explanation. "When this house was built, all wallpaper was imported from England. It was pretty costly, so once they put it on, it stayed on for quite a while. Besides, it was of good, enduring quality, and there wasn't a lot of city dirt and soot around in those days to soil it."

"You mean these little cherries made an ocean voyage?"

Happy shook his head. "I doubt it. It's the print underneath that did. Along about 1790, America started to manufacture her own wallpapers. You know, one of the first factories was here in Philadelphia."

"Well," Connie conceded, "I can understand why they wouldn't scrape between the first and second layers—and, from Lance, why Miss Calder didn't. But how about the intervening years?"

Happy got up and went over to the wall. With his fingernail, he began peeling along the ragged edge of the tan paper that encircled the cherry print. Connie munched on a liverwurst sandwich as she watched him.

"That's what I imagined," he said finally. "There are two layers of tan—"

"Both Miss Calder's," Connie interjected.

"And then another. A grim job of garlands. That was late nineteenth century." He held up his hand suddenly to stop Connie's next question. "Don't ask me why they didn't scrape between that and the cherries. I don't know. But I'll hazard a guess. The neighborhood was already on the downgrade.

"Once this was a fashionable residential section, but the families moved uptown around Rittenhouse Square and then out into the suburbs, and this part of town became scrum-dum. Mr. Calder told me this place degenerated into a cheap boardinghouse, then it was used as a warehouse for a publishing firm until old Carrie moved back. She owned it, and got so little rent, she figured she might as well live in it."

"Oh, Hap, it must have been fun to have been a Colonial Calder!"

"Maybe," he conceded. "But if you had been the first Mrs. Calder, you'd have been plagued by bird-cage skirts and you'd have been cold. They didn't have central heating systems, remember?"

"I'm cold now." Connie shivered. A new oil burner was to be installed, replacing the antiquated coal furnace in the basement that was at present anything but efficient. The hall was decidedly chilly. "But if I'd been the first Mrs. Calder, I'd have had a roaring fire going."

Connie looked longingly through the archway

into the living room where a wide hearth yawned empty and black under a stately mantel. Once it had glowed with warmth and welcome.

Happy followed her glance speculatively. "I don't see why you can't have your fire, Connie."

"But, Hap, we have no logs—and no andirons."

"Logs, no. But wood we have to burn, so to speak." He indicated the pile of scrap lumber in one corner of the living room. "Where there's a carpenter, there's a pile of wood. They'd only cart this out, anyhow. And, as for andirons, if you insist, they're a simple matter."

Happy walked down the hall and disappeared through the rear door into the garden. Seconds later, he was back with four bricks cradled in his arms. "See what papa found? Where there are bricklayers, there are bricks."

"And where there is a visiting fireman, there shall be a fire?" Connie raised her brown eyes laughingly.

The fire caught quickly and blazed cheerily. "Come, sit," Happy invited, with a gallant gesture toward the floor. "We'll pretend to be a struggling young artist couple in a Paris garret, too poor to buy furniture."

Connie stretched her hands gratefully toward the comforting warmth of the crackling scrap wood and tried to decide whether or not to tell Happy the story of the missing Queens. Certainly he, if anyone, would know about possible secret hiding places in old houses. But she was afraid he would laugh at her. Like Mr. Calder, he would

Drake pointed menacingly toward the fireplace

be certain that the fate of the figurines was less dramatic than Maryanne Jessup insisted, or hoped. Undoubtedly he'd go along with the more sensible theory that Miss Calder had given them away as she had so many of her other possessions.

She was glad she had kept silent, for Lance strolled into the room, drinking milk from a bottle. "Hey, this heat feels good. Even my bones are frozen. May I join you?"

Connie moved over to allow him a place directly in front of the hearth. Then Happy, Connie, and Lance all moved over, for two of the workmen, enticed by the fragrant aroma of the burning wood, came downstairs to enjoy an after-lunch cigarette.

It became a merry group. The workmen regaled them with hilarious tales of other reconstruction jobs they had done in the area. Everyone laughed. And then the jollity ended abruptly.

"Who did this?"

At the apoplectic demand behind them, they swung around. Glaring at them from under the archway was Andrew Drake, office manager for the Calder Insurance Company. His pudgy face was white and stormy as he pointed menacingly toward the fireplace. His paunchy body seemed to quiver all over.

"Who did this?" he repeated.

Connie had to suppress a desire to giggle. He reminded her exactly of a man asking a litter of small puppies which one had chewed the shoe.

"I did it," Happy admitted.

"I suggested it," Connie added.

"An open fire should not have been started without my permission," Drake said pompously. "Do you realize, my girl, that if the flue hadn't worked, your suggestion might have resulted in irreparable loss, not only to Mr. Calder, but—"

"I'm not a fool, Drake," Happy said, jumping to his feet and moving protectingly in front of Connie. She had never seen him angry before. This was a new side of Happy Wallace. "I checked that flue yesterday, or I wouldn't have started the fire."

Then Lance also rose, saying, "And may I remind you that Miss Blair is a young lady. That's hardly the way to address a lady."

Connie turned in amazement. She never associated such gallantry with Lance Hurley. It was the sort of remark Mr. Calder might have made, calmly, but with a knife-sharp quality that meant business.

"Well . . . I . . . well . . . perhaps I *was* a little hasty . . ."

The office manager was nonplused. Lance's remark obviously upset him. And, by losing his temper, he realized that he had been rude, not only to Connie, but to men not much his junior. He was completely embarrassed as he mumbled the grudging retraction. But Connie sensed that she, as the principal reason for his discomfort, had unwittingly made an enemy of Andrew Drake.

CHAPTER 3

Worth of an Inheritance

IN SPITE of Happy's fire, the old house had grown uncomfortably cold by midafternoon.

"That tired old furnace can't keep up with the weather any more," one of the carpenters remarked, passing through the hall. "I think we'd better quit soon before we all turn blue."

Connie nodded, and about four o'clock, by mutual consent, everyone on the job agreed to call it a day. Connie muffled her coat around her and left with the rest. For her, it was a perfect point at which to stop work, since she had finished the tracing and already transferred it to her watercolor block. To get out her painting equipment for the little remaining time would have been just so much wasted effort.

The snow had stopped. On Fifth Street, under the passing traffic, it was turning to slush that reminded Connie of the brown sugar and vinegar her mother used to glaze baked ham. Glad that her loafers and heavy socks would keep her feet dry, she started across Independence Square.

People in the neighboring offices were still at work, and Connie had the Square to herself. In the premature dusk, it had taken on the silence that comes with snowfall. Later, the snow on the paths would be marred by homeward-bound pass-ers-by, but now it was still pristine, clean, and beautiful. Under the darkening sky, the Square seemed to be momentarily resting.

After the excitement of Maryanne and the figurines, and Mr. Drake and the fire, it was relaxing just to walk through the Square. Connie smiled at the snow turban the statue of Commodore John Barry was wearing. It made the Revolutionary naval hero look like a Russian Cossack.

Passing Independence Hall, it occurred to her that she had never seen the Liberty Bell. Like so many Philadelphians, she had neglected it, leaving it to tourists from far places. The double doors of the State House facing the Square were unlocked. Connie pushed one open and walked in. The Hall was empty of visitors and in its bare setting the bell looked solemn, substantial, and alone. Connie stared at the historic crack for a minute or two, feeling a sort of reverent peace. Then she went out the front door onto Chestnut Street.

Here the quiet of the past ended abruptly. Shoppers crowded the pavements and many of the lighted store windows were already decorated for Christmas, although Thanksgiving had just passed. In one of Gimbel's windows a glittering sleigh was piled high with gaily wrapped packages and, outside the store, the tingling music of "Jingle Bells" spilled out over the heads of the crowd from some unseen source.

In the next block the gloomy façades of the Court building and Federal Reserve Bank made a somber contrast to Gimbel's festivity and she hurried by them to where more lighted windows brightened the early-winter evening.

Wanamaker's was exceedingly rewarding, with animated scenes from Dickens' *Christmas Carol*. Connie spent some time viewing each window and then crossed Juniper Street, anticipating the handsome merchandise in Caldwell's, the famous jeweler. But once in front of the store, she hardly saw the diamonds, the chinaware, the clocks and silver trophy cups. One thing only claimed her attention: a single figure of a porcelain shepherdess and the neatly lettered card beneath it.

Sèvres . . . $500.

One Sèvres figurine valued at five hundred dollars! Why, a matched collection of six must be worth thousands! No wonder Maryanne wanted to track them down.

As usual, Connie arrived at the apartment before Aunt Bet. She took the mail from the box and sorted it on the way upstairs. There was one letter for her . . . from Kit.

Kicking off her wet loafers, but without bothering to remove her coat, she flopped on the sofa and tore open the envelope. "Connie, lamb," she read, "I'm writing from my desk while the hardware business is temporarily slack . . ."

Normally, news from home was a high spot in Connie's day, but halfway through the neatly typed pages she realized that not a word beyond Kit's first sentence had penetrated her consciousness. Her mind was still too engrossed with Maryanne Jessup.

Valuable as the Queens might turn out to be, Maryanne's interest in tracking them down was more than monetary, Connie decided. The tall woman in the mink coat and peculiar hat was a sentimentalist.

"Aunt Carrie used to let me hold them," Connie remembered her having told Mr. Calder. "I knew their names and their histories . . ."

Yes, to Maryanne, the figurines had been real, honest-to-goodness people just like any small girl's dolls. Probably Mr. Calder couldn't understand this little-girl-like love, nor the reason behind Maryanne's conviction that they were still around somewhere waiting for her. But to Connie, it was perfectly evident. Maryanne refused to face up to the fact that Miss Calder had betrayed her by giving away the friends of her childhood.

Pathetically, all Maryanne's efforts to locate the cherished figurines were being balked by the easily acceptable theory that they had suffered a fate similar to the coffee service and other heirlooms.

The apartment-house lobby buzzer jolted Connie out of her reverie. Rising quickly, she pressed the button that released the lock on the downstairs door. Aunt Bet must have forgotten her key.

But Connie was wrong. The person who appeared presently at the top of the two-flight staircase when Connie opened the door was Earle Filmore.

"Good evening, Constance," he greeted, puffing slightly from exertion as he removed his hat. "Elizabeth home yet?"

Connie shook her head and smiled. His use of their full Christian names always amused her. It was one of the eccentricities which made the genial, pint-sized dilettante something of a character. A musician by profession, he dabbled in all things artistic, and this neighbor and long-time friend of her aunt had a natural politeness and formal manner of address that would have fitted the most sedate Victorian salon.

"No? . . . Then I'll trot along. Just dropped by to see about digging up a bridge game for tonight. Tell Elizabeth to call me."

"Mr. Filmore! Wait!" Connie cried out on sudden impulse. "Please come in and sit down. I have something to ask you."

Earle Filmore looked surprised, then flattered. "Well, Constance"—he beamed—"it isn't often a pretty young damsel asks my advice. What is your problem?"

Connie settled him in the most comfortable

armchair, then sat down again on the sofa opposite. "Have you ever heard of porcelain called Sèvres?"

"Sèvres," he repeated. "But of course. Exquisite."

"And did you ever hear of six Sèvres queens?"

"Six queens? Sèvres? Now, let me think. Yes, a set of six. I have heard of them, Constance. A friend of mine, an art dealer, appraised them not long ago."

"For a Miss Calder?"

"I can't recall the woman's name. But she lived on Fifth Street."

"That's the one!" Connie exclaimed. "Are they valuable, Mr. Filmore?"

He laughed. "Valuable! That's why I remember them so distinctly. This woman—Miss Calder —intended having them insured, but when she learned how much it would cost, she said she would save the money on premiums and protect them herself. Is that logic? Seems to me the more expensive things are, the more they should be insured."

Connie skipped Mr. Filmore's opinion on insurance. Saving money was typical of what she had heard about old Miss Calder, and she wanted to find out more about the statuettes themselves.

"What were the Queens like, Mr. Filmore? Did your friend tell you?"

"Yes, a little." He tapped the table at his elbow thoughtfully. "One was Boadicea, Queen of the Ancient Britons. Another was Clothilde. She was the wife of Clovis, King of the Franks, whom she converted to Christianity. Then there was Blanche of Castile, the Queen of Louis VIII of France.

"Then—oh, yes—there was Theodora, the consort of one of the Byzantine emperors. She left a great deal to be desired as to character, but she *was* famous—or infamous. And—well, I can't remember the rest of the names.

"They were about eight inches tall and stood on round, hollow pedestals about four inches in diameter. But the interesting thing about the set was their crowns. Each wore a crown of a special ruby hue never before or never afterward produced. This unusual set, portraying famous queens of history, was extremely valuable. My friend offered a small fortune for them at the appraisal but was turned down. Miss Calder said they weren't for sale. By the way," he asked suddenly, "what do you know about the Queens?"

"Nothing," Connie admitted. "I'm working in Miss Calder's old house. I've heard of them, that's all. I was just trying to visualize them."

It was true. Actually she didn't *know* anything about them, and she didn't want to divulge any of the Calder family's private affairs. She hoped he would not query her further. He didn't. Fortunately, his interest now was on more mundane matters.

"I'm famished," he announced. "When Elizabeth comes in, tell her to give me a ring."

After he had gone, Connie picked up Kit's letter. Filing away for possible future use the information that Mr. Filmore had given her, she turned her thoughts to news of the family.

Everyone was well enough. Ruggles, the cocker spaniel, had just recovered from a touch of tonsillitis. Toby had fallen out of a tree and sprained his wrist, but it was the left one and didn't interfere with his activities too greatly. Her mother had been elected president of the Women's Auxiliary at church. The rest concerned plans for the Christmas holiday.

Again the buzzer sounded from the lobby, and again she pressed the button that unlocked the door. This time it was surely Aunt Bet. But the buzzer persisted, so apparently she had been wrong again. Whoever was downstairs wanted to talk, not come up. She lifted the receiver from the house phone and said politely, "Yes?"

"Connie?" Happy's voice came back promptly. "Don't you think it might be a bright idea to find out who's down here before you let them, or it, in? Could be a trained seal or—"

"Oh, Happy," Connie interrupted, laughing. "Come on up."

"Nope. I haven't time. I just want you to do me a favor."

"Oh. What's the favor?"

"Wear a skirt to work tomorrow."

"A skirt? Don't you approve of jeans?"

"Uh-huh. But not when I'm taking you to lunch. After all, I owe you a hard-boiled egg."

Connie gulped. "Is—is this an invitation?"

"Yes, engraved and with R.S.V.P. in the lower left-hand corner. How about it, Connie?" He sounded serious now. "I know a place you'll like. You can play Miss Colonial Somebody-or-other."

"Why, I'd—I'd love to go, Happy!" Connie accepted graciously and enthusiastically, her thoughts already on what she would wear. She decided on her gray wool. She could cover it with a smock while working.

"Great! I won't be surveying tomorrow at the house, but I'll pick you up there at five after twelve . . ." He paused for a few seconds and then continued, "I'm borrowing my roommate's car. Watch for it on the dot, because I'll never find a place to park."

"But how will I know it?"

"It's a green Buick convertible, 1950 vintage. You can't possibly miss it. And because the top won't go up any more, bring something to cover you if it's raining or snowing."

"Clear tomorrow," Connie predicted lightly. "I can tell by the sky."

"Okay, then, be at the curb. Five after twelve sharp. Uh-oh! Here's a smart-looking gal coming up the front steps with a key in her hand. Must be your aunt. I'll introduce myself."

Connie hung up and ran to greet Elizabeth Easton at the stair landing. There was no denying her excitement and the sparkle in her eyes.

"Guess what, Aunt Bet? Happy just asked me for a date!"

CHAPTER 4

Locked in the Cellar

AT PRECISELY five minutes past twelve Connie stationed herself on the pavement outside the Calder mansion to watch for Happy. Maryanne Jessup had been lucky yesterday to find a parking place. Today there were two cars parked at the curb where the station wagon had been: a small foreign roadster and a black sedan.

Happy was prompt. Connie had been waiting only a minute or two when she saw the green Buick, top down, round the nearby corner and join the steady stream of traffic on Fifth Street. She waved and ran out between the parked cars. As Happy stopped to let her in, the driver in the car behind immediately blew his horn.

"Creeps!" Happy exclaimed in annoyance. "That's the machine age for you. Hurry! Hurry! Hurry!"

"Maybe he happens to be in a hurry," Connie ventured as they started forward.

"No, he's not. It's just a habit."

"How do you know?"

Happy looked at her and grinned. "I don't. I just like to argue. Also I like the way the sun is shining on your shining hair."

For a few blocks they rode in silence and then Happy turned right and headed for the river. The neighborhood became more dreary and, in Connie's opinion, less and less likely of producing anything resembling a decent tearoom. They were in a commercial district of the city that had given itself over to third- and fourth-rate wholesale establishments, warehouses, and small businesses.

The streets were choked with trucks of all sizes, many illegally parked and causing single-line traffic to crawl along the narrow Philadelphia arteries.

"Happy, where are you taking me?"

"Keep calm," he told her. "We're almost there."

Connie didn't reply, but she wondered if she could ever eat in this atmosphere. The air was redolent with a combination of smells. There was the sick-sweet odor from a candy factory mingled with decayed fruit and bilge from the nearby river shipping.

They turned south into Second Street and Happy veered into a parking lot next to a restaurant supply store where chrome coffee urns, stools, and tables were displayed behind murky windows.

"Look back of you, Connie," Happy directed. "Not around."

Connie obeyed and her misgivings vanished. Not fifty feet away was a tiny cobblestoned alley about ten feet wide. On either side of the narrow lane were almost identical rows of the trimmest little houses she had ever seen. In contrast to the rest of the neighborhood, they were almost unbelievable.

"Hap!" she cried in delight, looking up at the street sign. "It's Elfreth's Alley, isn't it? I've heard of it, but I've never been here. I didn't even know where it was."

Happy nodded and took her arm. "Few people do, yet it's the oldest *street* in America. The tearoom's in the middle of the block."

"Do we have to go right in? Couldn't we walk a bit first?"

"Why, sure," Happy agreed. "But except for a little court, this is it."

The thirty-three little houses were in fairly good repair and most of them were occupied. Many had window boxes which Connie pictured filled with gay petunias or geraniums in summer. Some had artistic baskets hanging on the door for mail. As she and Happy walked slowly along, Connie caught glimpses of attractively furnished interiors through the windows that still boasted some pre-Revolutionary hand-blown glass.

"This is really a landmark, Happy. Who lived

here originally?" Connie asked, thrilled with the new site of something old and historical.

"Oh, the butcher, the baker, the candlestick maker. And Ben Franklin."

They reached the entrance to Bladen's Court, a tiny shoot off the main alley, not more than sixty feet long, and ending at what once had been a public water pump. Beside the pump was a house with a vine-covered balcony.

"Oh, Hap, look at that!" Connie exclaimed, pointing. "Isn't it adorable?"

"That was known as a spinning balcony. Women took their wheels out on them to get the air while they worked. And the hum of the loom had no automobile horn blowers to contend with . . ."

"You mean our friend on Fifth Street?"

"Like him," Happy agreed. "Let's eat."

Although they had passed no one on their tour of the alley, the tearoom was crowded. "I'll have a table for you shortly," the hostess told Happy. "Why not look around the cellar while you're waiting? Most visitors like to."

Happy led the way down a winding stair, but neither the cellar which was lighted by an area-way leading to the street, nor the antiques displayed there, were particularly exciting. The thing that caught Connie's interest was a brick archway that led into another room, much smaller than the main cellar.

"What was that room used for?" she asked.

Happy smiled tolerantly. "That was the cold

room where they kept perishable foods and stuff
before mechanical refrigeration was invented.
But I know what you're thinking, Miss Mystery.
You've got it all nicely catalogued as a secret hiding place for Colonial valuables."

"Well, it wouldn't have been such a bad one
at that," Connie defended herself, somewhat
lamely. Happy had been so right in interpreting
her thoughts. The moment she had spied the
archway, she recalled Mr. Calder's remark—that
Maryanne was obsessed with the idea of secret
hiding places in old houses.

"I imagine you're not too far wrong, Connie,"
Happy admitted. "I was teasing. Occasionally
these old cellars did have secret hiding places.
Sometimes just a few loose bricks. Sometimes
pretty elaborate. I suppose it was all part of the
unsettled times—"

"Happy," Connie interrupted, her mind
racing, "has the Calder house a cold room?"

"Yep. Behind the furnace."

As quickly as she could, she told Happy a little
about the figurines, but he merely laughed.
"Those things! Drake was hunting them the first
day I came to work."

"But, Hap, did he look in the cold room?"

"That's where he started. The most obvious
place. And you can bet your lily-white hands
he'd have found them if they'd been there."

Connie felt deflated and was glad when the
hostess called from the head of the stairs that
their table was ready.

Connie had intended taking the least expensive lunch. From the things Happy had said, and the fact that he was working to pay part of his tuition, she knew he hadn't much extra money. But the tearoom offered only two selections and they were both the same price. Connie ordered the sandwich platter and Happy took the meat loaf.

"I won't be on Fifth Street the rest of the week," he told her while they were waiting to be served. "We're on charette."

"On what?"

"Charette. It's a term we use at school—the name for a little French cart the architectural students in Paris used to carry their big drawing boards around in. Now we apply the word to the final days of a design problem when we're working day and night to meet the deadline. The drawings have to be finished by five o'clock Saturday."

Connie waited, hoping he might ask her for another date later Saturday. When he didn't, she asked casually, "Who'll do the surveying while you're on charette?"

"Butterfield."

"Butterfield?" Connie gasped. She couldn't have been more surprised if he had said her spaniel Ruggles. To her, Mr. Butterfield was just a handyman for the construction company. His main job was seeing that the tools were all accounted for and that the house was locked up at night after the workmen left.

Happy laughed at her amazement. "Butterfield's a funny old goat, Connie. He's really a graduate engineer, gone to seed . . . Ah, at long last, food!"

The waitress put their plates in front of them and Happy looked at his watch. "I hate to have to rush, Connie, but I've got to hurry back to the campus. Mind if we just eat and run?"

Getting lunch over as soon as possible didn't include much conversation. They ate in silence, and twenty minutes later Happy dropped her back at the house on Fifth Street.

Lance and all the workmen were busy on the second floor. Connie had the hall to herself all afternoon. With no interruptions, she was able to finish her painting of the cherry print by four-thirty. She made a large cross on the wall beside it to indicate that she had completed this particular paper. Then, covering her water-color block with tracing paper to keep it clean, she laid it together with her paintbox on the window sill beside one of the flashlights the electricians were forever leaving all over the place. On impulse, she picked up the light and tucked it under her arm.

Although Happy had pooh-poohed the idea of a secret hiding place in the cold cellar, Connie decided to make sure. Even if she didn't find it, she might discover some other clue that Mr. Drake had missed. Furthermore, it would be fun to explore the cellar and she had half an hour until quitting time. There was no more she could do at the moment, for the cherry print had to soak overnight before it could be peeled off and she could begin on the paper underneath.

The knob was missing from the cellar door at the rear of the hall. A large barrel bolt had been installed to keep it shut. Connie slid the bolt and started down the steep stairs. Although the leaky old furnace gave off a slight illumination, she was glad she had brought along the flashlight. Beside the old heater, the new oil burner stood, bright and shiny, waiting to be connected.

She noticed immediately that the cellar was frightfully untidy. All along the stone wall facing the steps were stacks and stacks of newspapers, and the floor everywhere was littered with trash. Most of it was a recent accumulation, debris from the remodeling that had been thrown there to get it out of the way. The rest evidently was Miss Calder's household castoffs: a glass lamp shade, pink and hideous; a breadboard, cracked in two; a chair, minus one leg.

Midway down the cellar an electric light dangled from a frayed cord. It was an old-fashioned, unfrosted bulb in a tarnished brass socket controlled by a pull chain. Connie walked over and pulled the chain, but the ancient bulb did not respond.

Using her flashlight, she played it along the walls in search of the entrance to the cold room. She found it quite easily, as Happy had told her, behind the furnace—a low, bricked arch similar to the one in the tearoom.

For a moment she hesitated. What if there were mice in there—or, worse, rats? She kicked at the side wall and waited, listening for sounds of frightened scurrying. When she heard nothing, she stooped and went in, guided by the flashlight.

The room was unexpectedly small, about seven feet square she judged. The space to the left of the arch was lined with whitewashed wooden shelves. But nothing was stored there now and the shelves were completely bare. The rest of the room was equally empty and disappointing. It was entirely brick-lined, even the ceiling, but there was no indication of a secret hiding place.

Leaving the room, she went back to the main cellar and carefully investigated the walls. Happy might have been wrong about the location or existence of a secret hiding place. But the stone walls and brick floor were solid and unrevealing. Finally, she moved the stacks of papers in the hope of uncovering a sort of trap door. Again she was disappointed, but as she pushed the papers back into place, she saw that they had been saved with a purpose.

A label on the first stack, lettered in pencil on a scrap of cheap stationery, read: LINDBERGH'S FLIGHT. On the second: WORLD WAR II. On the third: DEATH NOTICES OF INTEREST.

Connie skipped the rest and pulled the top paper from the second stack. The headline interested her:

PRESIDENT ROOSEVELT SAYS AMERICA WILL NOT GO TO WAR.

It was dated 1939. She began leafing through, wondering what other erroneous forecasts it contained, but it was the advertising on the inside pages that claimed her attention.

NEW MODEL CHEVROLET—$582.50 . . . ROUND TRIP TO BERMUDA—$60.00 and up . . . FULL-COURSE DINNERS—65¢.

Fascinated by the low prices, Connie read on. And then, without warning, the flashlight dimmed and went dead.

Picking up the paper, she carried it over to the furnace and spread it on the floor where there was just enough glow to see by. It was a standing joke with the family in Meadowbrook that when Connie started reading anything, the end of the world couldn't take her mind from it. But now, as she bent down, she was conscious of a peculiar quiet in the house above her. The noise of hammering and sawing, which had become so familiar that she hardly ever noticed them, had stopped. She glanced at her watch. It was five-thirty. Of course it was quiet; all the workmen had gone home.

How absent-minded can you be? she chided herself as she groped her way up the steps. And she had promised to put the potatoes in to bake, so that she and Aunt Bet could have an early dinner and Aunt Bet could get to her concert on time.

At the top of the steps, Connie pushed against the door. It would not open. She tried it again, with more force this time. Still it did not budge.

Someone, she realized in a sudden moment of panic, had slipped the bolt. She was locked in!

CHAPTER 5

A Cozy Chat

"HELP, somebody! Help! It's Connie Blair. I'm locked in the cellar!"

Certainly if any of the workmen were still upstairs, they were bound to hear her. Connie waited, listening for footsteps coming in answer to her cries. But beyond the bolted door there was no sound, nothing but an overpowering silence.

Again she called and again she pounded, with such vigor this time that she bruised her fists. Everyone was gone! She was completely alone and the house, she supposed, was dark, for there was not even a streak of light along the crack at the bottom of the door.

But where was Mr. Butterfield? His only real job began after the workmen had left. Surely it took him longer than half an hour to gather up all the tools, stow them away in the supply room, and lock the house. However, it would be just her luck that this evening he had skimped his duties in order to get away early.

That must be it! He'd been in a hurry, and seeing the cellar door opened, he'd bolted it without bothering to ask if anyone were down there. But the fact that Mr. Butterfield, unknowingly, had locked her in did not mitigate matters.

And her coat? Hadn't he seen her coat lying on the bench in the hall? Wasn't that significant that she was somewhere in the house? Why hadn't he looked for her, or at least called?

All of this was of no consequence, Connie forced herself to realize. The question of the moment, to which she had no answer, was whether or not Mr. Butterfield was coming back before morning.

Connie slumped down on the top step. The prospect of spending the night in that gloomy, dark cellar with only Miss Calder's old newspapers and the old coal furnace for company was anything but cheerful. What an impulsive idiot she had been not to tell someone that she was going into the cellar!

And Aunt Bet! Aunt Bet would be frantic when she didn't come home. But there was a glimmer of comfort in thinking about Aunt Bet. Conceivably Aunt Bet might contact Happy when she failed to appear for dinner. He was the only person associated with Connie at the Calder

"Help! I'm locked in the cellar."

mansion whom her aunt had met. And Happy, knowing Connie's interest in the cold room at Elfreth's Alley and her obvious curiosity, might figure out the predicament . . .

But that was too long a chance. Aunt Bet, more likely, would call the police. And the police probably would start their search by getting in touch with Mr. Calder. And Mr. Calder probably would telephone Mr. Drake . . .

After the fireplace episode, the last person on earth Connie wanted to discover her present plight was Drake.

If Mr. Butterfield would only return and let her out quietly, without a lot of fuss and confusion! Wasn't there some reason for him to come back, she wondered, forcing herself to be calm.

The furnace! Along with his other chores, Butterfield tended the furnace, and furnaces had to be banked for the night. Connie had lived all her life with an oil burner and her knowledge of coal furnaces was practically nil, but the phrase "banked for the night" was familiar. More than being familiar, the phrase was definitely reassuring. She'd been in the cellar alone since four-thirty. Certainly Butterfield wouldn't have banked the fire before that time.

In a few short minutes which seemed an eternity to Connie, her mind raced, exploring other probabilities of escape. Suddenly, to her great elation, she heard footsteps in the hall. She jumped to her feet and called loudly:

"Mr. Butterfield! Mr. Butterfield! Let me out of here, please, before you do another thing!"

The door was unbolted immediately and Connie blinked to adjust her eyes to the glare of light from the hundred-and-fifty-watt bulb that hung, shadeless, from the hall ceiling.

"Oh, thank you, Mr. Butter—" But she didn't finish. The man who had released her was Andrew Drake.

"Well, Miss Blair!" he said acidly. "What's the meaning of *this?*"

"I . . . I . . ." Connie faltered. "I was in the basement and Mr. Butterfield locked me in by mistake."

"And what, may I ask, were you doing in the basement?"

Under his icy stare, Connie groped for an answer. She could have excused herself on the basis of her curiosity about the newspapers. But how was she to have known they were there in the first place? After all, Connie was not one to dissemble. Her mission in the basement was no crime, and suddenly she was annoyed that Mr. Drake was acting as though she had just committed some federal offense. Mustering her dignity, she said simply: "I was looking for the figurines, Mr. Drake. Or a possible clue to their whereabouts."

The man's manner changed abruptly. His paunchy body started to quiver, as it had yesterday when he had been so incensed about the fire. "The figurines!" he fairly exploded, his voice rising. "Miss Blair, the figurines are none of your business! Furthermore, I have made a thorough search for them, and I am a thorough man. If they were here, neither they, nor, as you put it, 'a clue to their whereabouts' would have escaped me. They were given away and that's that!"

"I'm sorry, Mr. Drake," Connie apologized, momentarily frightened by his menacing tone. "I didn't mean to imply you were negligent."

"Well, that's what it amounts to. And if I hadn't stopped by to check the outlets and make sure that the electricians installed them in the right places, you'd have spent the night in the cellar. And it would have served you right!"

Connie didn't venture her conjecture that Mr. Butterfield probably would have come back to stoke the furnace. Her main objective was to get away from Mr. Drake. He was not only an arrogant man, but became uncontrollably fiery when either his authority or his integrity was questioned. She had seen it happen twice now.

"I must go home. My aunt may be worried . . ." She picked up her coat, wondering again why Mr. Butterfield had not noticed it lying on the bench, threw it across her shoulders, and started toward the door.

"Miss Blair—"

"Yes, Mr. Drake?" Connie paused, but did not turn around.

"I didn't mean to . . . er . . . blow my top. It's just that this affair of Miss Calder's will, and the Queens in particular, has me very much distressed. I went to work for Montgomery Calder's firm as an office boy, and over the years, I've become rather close to the family. I hate to see such dissent among them, especially this unpleasantness between Maryanne and Montgomery."

Connie turned. Mr. Drake had sat down on the bench and his anger of a moment ago was under control. Very definitely he wanted to talk.

Along with his arrogance, he's a gossip, Connie realized, smiling to herself and feeling in control of the situation. He doesn't like me, but he's willing to forget that fact in favor of a cozy chat about the Calders.

Connie, too, sat down. She wasn't averse to learning more about the family. Any shred of information might reveal a clue to the fate of the figurines. Glancing at her watch, she decided Aunt Bet would not yet have begun to worry and was eating her dinner alone, thinking Connie had been delayed at the job as she occasionally was.

"Did you know Miss Calder, too, Mr. Drake?" Connie asked, accepting his opening for a discussion. "What kind of person was she?"

"I knew the old lady very well, Miss Blair. At Montgomery's request, I used to stop by every time I was in the neighborhood to see how she was and if she needed any advice on her securities and the like. She was a strong-willed woman, Miss Blair, and she had her good points and her bad. She was penny-pinching to a fault and yet, at the same time, she could be generous. There was no accounting for what she did. If anyone crossed her, she could be intensely disagreeable and unforgiving, but she was proud of her family, and with few exceptions, fond of them all, especially of Maryanne and Montgomery. They were her favorites."

"But, Mr. Drake," Connie interposed, frowning, "if Miss Calder liked Maryanne, why would she hurt her by giving the Queens to someone else? It doesn't make sense."

Mr. Drake shrugged. "Possibly not, but it's what happened. Their disappearance followed too closely the pattern of the coffee set and the other valuables. Nellie, the housemaid, returned from her Thursday afternoon off and they were gone. That was only three days before the old lady died."

"But couldn't a thief have broken in while Nellie was out?"

"Not a chance," Mr. Drake replied. "We'd all worried about that eventuality for years and had been urging her to insure her valuables, but she maintained that it was too expensive. However, had the figurines been stolen, Miss Calder would have reported it immediately to the police. She wasn't sick, you know, and she wasn't senile. She passed away in her sleep. Cardiac, they told us."

The repetition of the plural "we" and "us" amused Connie. It tied in with the way he savored Montgomery Calder's first name. It was easy now to sense a definite purpose in Mr.

Drake's clubby little chat: he wanted to impress her with his connections with the Calder family.

"Since Maryanne was in Europe and Montgomery was south, fishing, I took care of the funeral arrangements. The same morning I went down to make the arrangements," he went on with a casualness that Connie was sure belied his real feeling of importance, "Nellie told me about the Queens."

"Oh, you mean no one knew they were gone until then?"

"No one but Nellie."

"Goodness!" Connie exclaimed, blinking. "Nellie really had a Heaven-sent chance to spirit them away for herself before you arrived, didn't she? And with the affairs of the coffee service and other stuff to set a precedent—"

"You suspect Nellie of *stealing* them?" Mr. Blake came as near to laughing as Connie believed he was capable. "Oh, mercy no! Nellie is the soul of honesty. Her only interest was the garden. She tended it religiously. Even bought shrubs and bushes from her own meager wages. Miss Calder let her amuse herself, since it was cheaper than hiring a gardener."

Connie felt contrite. She hadn't meant to brand Nellie as a criminal. Her outburst had been purely spontaneous because, at the moment, the maid's opportunity to have taken the figurines had been so startling.

"I shouldn't have said that, Mr. Drake," she apologized. "And now I must be going."

She stood up, noting that one of the the work-men had fastened a wet sponge on the wall over the cherry print and that her water-color block and paintbox were no longer on the window sill. Undoubtedly Mr. Butterfield had gathered them up and put them in the supply room while she was in the basement.

"As I said before, Miss Blair," Mr. Drake sighed, following her to the door, "this affair of the Queens is distressing to all of us. When I made my search of the house, the workmen were all agog at the mystery, but they have forgotten it recently. There's no point in having it revived and bruited about again."

"Meaning . . . Mr. Drake?"

"That we keep this little incident of your being in the basement, most particularly because of what you were doing in the basement, strictly between the two of us."

"Of course, Mr. Drake. I won't mention it to a soul. Not even to Mr. Butterfield." If she decided to continue her search for the Queens, she'd have a better chance of finding them if no one knew what she was up to. It wasn't always the safest way, but it had paid off in the past.

"And you forget the entire incident, too, Miss Blair," Mr. Drake called after her as she started down the steps. "The figurines were given away —possibly to someone none of us knows."

Connie hailed a passing cab, gave the driver the address of the apartment, and settled back on the seat, smiling to herself. Drake was so sure of himself, so positive that the figurines could not have escaped his notice.

Also, he was obviously pleased with the friendly chat which he evidently considered had established his position with the Calder family and, at the same time, disposed of the mystery of the Queens.

As the taxi jolted to a stop at a busy intersection, it jostled Connie's train of thought. Was she on the wrong track about Andrew Drake and the little chat?

Could the underlying aim of his professed loyalty to the Calders have been an attempt to throw her off the scent? Did he know more about the figurines than he was admitting? Had he possibly come across them in his search and taken them for himself? In that event, he would have every reason not to want their disappearance discussed further. His move would be to foster the deceptive theory that they simply had been given away—even to his exoneration of Nellie.

"I'm jumping to conclusions again!" Connie scolded herself, remembering her outburst about the maid.

But despite herself, she couldn't help wondering about Drake. Of one thing she was positive— no matter what the purpose behind it had been, Drake's declaration that Nellie was "the soul of honesty" had been sincere.

"We're here, miss," the taxi driver told her over his shoulder. "Isn't this the address you gave me?"

CHAPTER 6

Kittens in the Chimney

"PHILADELPHIA weather," Connie said aloud to herself as she stepped out into the old Calder garden. "One day blizzards, the next blossoms."

It would be many a month before the trees began to bud, but today the sun was warm, almost springlike. Wednesday's snow had completely disappeared and the ground looked pleasantly moist.

Instead of going directly to the original outkitchen which was presently serving as a supply room to store the workmen's portable tools and materials, Connie decided to circle the garden. Although it was overgrown in places, she could discern the effects of years of tender care.

Gravel paths bordered the four sides and bisected the yard, making a cross with a sundial

58

at their intersection. At the far end, on the axis
of the main path, in direct line with the rear
door of the house, a niche provided the point of
interest in a high brick wall.

At each of the back corners stood identical,
cubicle outbuildings unused now, one formerly
the water well and pump house, the other possibly the tack room before the stables had been
demolished and the ground beyond sold for a
commercial building site. Between these squat
structures lay the flower bed which had been
Nellie's pride. Unlike the overgrown grass plots
which made the four quarters of the main yard,
this little stretch showed unmistakable signs of
recent cultivation.

To the left of the entire garden, a tall iron
fence with a center gate gave onto a narrow side
street which was little more than an alley. Par-
alleling the fence along the opposite side of the
yard, the high brick wall of the adjoining Fifth
Street property shut in the garden and connected
with the outkitchen, which, in turn, connected
with the main house.

A covered porch ran the length of the kitchen
and turned at right angles across the back of the
house. The rear door to the house and the gate
in the fence provided the only egress and ingress
to the garden.

As Connie went down the side path, she saw
the friendly red-faced policeman she sometimes
met in the Square. He was patrolling his beat
on the pavement outside the fence.

"Hello," he said genially, recognizing her at once. "So this is where you work? You must be an artist," he added, noting the smock she was wearing over her camel-colored skirt and blouse. Since her luncheon date yesterday with Happy, she had discarded the blue jeans. They weren't necessary any more, now that most of the plastering had been finished.

Connie told him briefly about her job, then explained, "I'm on my way to collect my materials, but I couldn't resist a look at the garden."

"You ought to see it in the spring. Miss Nellie sure made it pretty."

"Oh, you knew Nellie?" Connie asked perfunctorily.

The policeman nodded. "Yes. I always stopped to pass the time of day with her while she was out here gardening. Worked hard, old and frail as she was. Promised her I'd keep an eye on the place after she left. People swipe things sometimes, even dig up bushes, from an empty property like this was until they started fixing it up."

Connie smiled. "Did you ever catch a thief here?"

"Nope. Only person I ever seen here was a fellow planting bulbs over there one Saturday in October." He pointed with his night stick to the far corner of the flower bed. "Lucky he got 'em in when he did. Soon afterward, the ground started to freeze. Got a mighty early cold snap this year. Unusual."

"You're so right." Connie shivered. The

warmth of the sun had deceived her. It was too chilly to be out without a coat. "I'd better go—"

But the policeman interrupted her attempt to break away. "Miss Nellie told me about those bulbs before she left. Said she'd ordered them all the way from Holland, just special. Shows how she loved the garden, don't it, having 'em put in even if she wouldn't be here to enjoy 'em? In summer," he mused, "she'd bring a chair out and read catalogues about seeds and— Say, miss, your teeth are chatterin'. You'll catch your death."

"I'm afraid I will," Connie agreed emphatically. "But it was fun talking with you."

She waved good-by and jog-trotted across the garden to the supply room.

The character references on Nellie she had gotten thus inadvertently from both Mr. Drake and the policeman seemed to absolve the housemaid of any connection with the disappearance of the figurines. Little elderly ladies who pore over seed catalogues only commit crimes in detective novels, she decided. And in the light of a normal workaday morning, even Connie's suspicions of Mr. Drake were fading. Quite likely she was seeing crime where there was none.

As she reached for the door of the outkitchen, it was suddenly opened from the inside. Momentarily startled, Connie composed herself, and noticing the figure on the inside, said pleasantly, "Oh, good morning, Mr. Butterfield."

Her captor of the night before admitted her

to the welcome shelter of the room. Dressed as always in a pair of faded khaki trousers and a ragged sweater, he was a bouncy little man about fifty years old—Connie judged—with a truly handsome head of wavy, iron-gray hair that lent incongruous dignity to his workman's attire.

Looking up from the handsaw he was carrying, he smiled. "Good morning, Miss Blair. Hunting your artist materials?"

Connie nodded. "Are they here in the supply room?"

"Yes, I found them on the window sill last evening and locked them up for you. Drake was due here later, and you know how he is about neatness—a place for everything and everything in its place."

Connie thanked him politely. It was terribly tempting to tell him that along with the artists' materials, he had also locked up the artist. But she had promised Mr. Drake not to mention it, even to Mr. Butterfield, and she intended to keep her word.

Mr. Butterfield made no further comment, and as she turned to gather up her equipment, Connie glanced surreptitiously at his features. They were nice and even, finely chiseled. When he was young, he must have been quite attractive. It was a shame his teeth were in such poor condition. The poor soul probably couldn't afford a good dentist.

"Miss Blair," he said, turning suddenly.

Connie averted her stare and let the art materials remain on the shelf. "Yes, Mr. Butterfield."

"About last night. I'm sorry I locked you in the cellar. I was in a great hurry to get off and I didn't realize you were down there."

So Drake had told after all! And he was the one who had made the suggestion about keeping things mum. But it was, of course, typical of Drake. In her mind, Connie reconstructed the scene: Mr. Butterfield had returned to bank the fire while Drake was still inspecting the electric outlets. Drake couldn't resist letting him know that he, Drake, had apprehended and righted Butterfield's mistake.

The handyman seemed so genuinely sorry for what he had done that Connie decided not to embarrass him further by suggesting that he had been negligent in not noticing her coat. Probably in his "great hurry to be off" and his preoccupation with the art materials, it had skipped his attention.

"Don't apologize, Mr. Butterfield," Connie said graciously. "You didn't do it on purpose. I'm just surprised that Mr. Drake mentioned it. He made *me* promise not to."

"He made you promise not to?" Mr. Butterfield repeated, clearly puzzled. "But why, Miss Blair? What were you doing in the cellar?"

"Well, I—I—" Connie faltered, groping for the right thing to say and still not divulge her real reason for being in the cellar. Apparently Drake had broken only half his promise. He had not mentioned the figurines. She said evasively, "I was looking for something."

Mr. Butterfield didn't pursue the question. Instead, he glanced down at the saw and began meditatively to test the sharpness of the blade with his fingers. Finally he said slowly, as though arriving at a decision, "Perhaps Drake has his reasons, Miss Blair. And since I haven't mentioned the cellar incident to anyone else, suppose we keep it a secret between the three of us?"

"All right. Provided Mr. Drake hasn't already made it public."

"I doubt if he has. And I also think, and this is important—that it would be prudent not to let on you found out he told me. In effect, he broke a promise to you, and that's not cricket. He couldn't abide being caught in a breach of confidence, and he'd resent us for finding him out. Do you agree?"

Connie grinned. "I do, definitely."

Without replying, Mr. Butterfield turned and went out. Connie watched his retreating back speculatively. Today was the first time she'd had any real contact or prolonged conversation with him and it was difficult to figure out what sort of person he was, because he was so out of character, rather well-bred and educated for so menial a job. Happy had said the man had gone to seed. She wondered about his background, where he lived now and whether he had a family. He certainly was an enigma. But of one thing concerning him she was positive. He had the office manager sized up to a T.

Alone in the supply room, Connie closed the door. Then she looked around her. In its present state, littered with tools and equipment pertinent to the remodeling, it was humdrum, but as a memento of life in the past, it was fascinating.

Typical of Colonial houses in their time, there was no original kitchen inside the house, only a modernized addition made by cutting up the old rear pantry. All food preparation had been done in this separate building; its only connection with the main house a covered porch which ran along the rear of the main building.

It was a single room, not an overly large one, and its main feature was the huge walk-in fireplace still unobstructed by the shelving and workbenches that had been installed temporarily.

The inside walls were rough plaster. The ceiling beams were exposed and blackened by the smoke from many an earlier cooking chore. The heavy chestnut lintel over the fireplace opening was split along its length. Hand-wrought hooks still protruded where an array of simple cooking utensils had once hung.

A Dutch oven with an iron door flanked the fireplace opening to the right and inside the fireplace there once had been a heavy crane to hold the stewpots. Only its hinge pins remained, embedded in the side stones.

With half-closed eyes Connie could visualize

the crackling open fire, the Brunswick stew simmering in the black kettle, the haunch of meat slowly being revolved on a spit turned by the perspiring scullery maid, the smell of fresh bread baking in the oven.

Certainly there had been no push-button magic here, nor dining alcove a few feet away. The food had to be hustled in covered dishes along the porch and into the house. And after that, dish-washing without detergents. What a chore! Heating more kettles of water over the waning fire, scrubbing with sand and soap made at home from fat drippings.

Mentally exhausted from visualizing the labor, Connie set about gathering up her water-color block, her paints and brushes. As she was about to fill the tin pan she used for water from the old-fashioned hand pump in the stone sink, she became conscious of a queer noise, a sort of soft cooing.

It was eerie, alone in the room. Maybe the old house had a private ghost. Then she scolded herself for being a sissy. It must be a dove, a dove in the eaves outside. But as she listened more closely, she was aware that the strange cooing was not coming from outside but from within the room.

"From the fireplace!" Connie blurted aloud.

Could it be a bird, trapped there and hurt? She loved birds for themselves, but always had been timid about their flutter at close range. However, the noise had to be investigated.

Laying the pan aside, she walked to the hearth. Here the sound was quite distinct. Looking up into the blackened interior of the chimney, Connie could see nothing. She needed a flashlight. She found one on the bench beside an assortment of tools.

Going back to the hearth, she flashed the light above her head. Nothing rewarded her upward gaze, however, but the smoke shelf, a large projection across the rear of the chimney wall built to prevent downdrafts from blowing smoke back into the room. Whatever was making the noise was on the smoke shelf or above it. Returning to the room, she found an empty wooden nail keg which she tested to see if it would hold her weight. Satisfied that it was amply strong, she hauled it into the fireplace and climbed on top. Even then her head was just short of the ledge. Even in the beam of the flashlight, she could not see the top of the shelf.

"Today I should have worn my jeans," she berated herself as she bent her knee and inserted the toe of her alligator pump into the rough rock of the chimney to give herself a push upward. Catching the edge of the smoke shelf, and supported by her foot, she formed a human wedge in the chimney. By a series of curious wriggles, she was able to get her elbow precariously on the shelf with one leg dangling free.

"Miss Blair!"

Surprised by the unexpected voice, Connie lost her insecure grip and dropped back to the hearth, missing the nail keg by inches. Mr. Butterfield was standing in the center of the room, looking appalled.

"How did you know I was up there?" Connie demanded, her feet stinging from the sudden impact on her high heels. It was annoying to have her rescue mission interrupted.

"Your foot was hanging down. But what on earth were you doing up the chimney?"

It must have been ludicrous, she thought, but she was glad she didn't have to be evasive again about her appearance in strange places. "There's something alive up there, Mr. Butterfield. It's making a noise, like something in trouble. If you'll give me a boost, I'll try—"

"You'll do no such thing!" he said emphatically. "Look at you! You're covered with soot. You'll hurt yourself. If there's any rescuing to be done, I'll do it."

He brushed her aside, grabbed the flashlight from her hand, and without bothering to step on the nail keg, used the iron crane hinge pin to hoist himself. Connie marveled at his agility.

"It's kittens," he announced a few seconds later. "A mother cat with a litter."

"Of course!" Connie exclaimed. "The cooing I heard was mewing."

"They can't stay up here. Stand below me, Miss Blair, and I'll hand them down to you."

"Won't the mother cat object?" Connie asked.

"No, she seems a friendly soul. And she looks half starved."

"All right, but the babies will need a bed. Wait until I find something to put them in."

Under the table where she had left the water pan, Connie spied a cardboard carton half filled with coils of wire which she dumped unceremoniously on the floor. She dragged the carton over to the hearth.

One by one, Mr. Butterfield handed her the kittens. The first was all black, the second black with a white circle around its neck like a collar. They couldn't have been more than a few days old.

"This one's a girl," Mr. Butterfield called down as he passed her the third tiny, furry ball. "All tricolor cats are females."

Connie tucked the little creature in between the first two. Its body was predominantly black, but its wizened face was a comical combination of white and orange divided directly down the middle.

The fourth was mostly white with orange stripings and the fifth was mostly orange with a white blaze on its nose.

"It's a gay litter." Connie laughed, watching them milling about in the box, their toenails making tiny scratching noises against the cardboard bottom.

"Here comes Ma," Mr. Butterfield advised. Connie held up both hands which were filled immediately with a remarkably large and emaciatedly thin cat who had no claim to distinction whatsoever except her size. She was plain tiger.

Connie deposited the mother cat with her brood and pulled the carton from the hearth to a dark corner of the room where the kittens would be in dim light until after their eyes opened.

"We'll have to get Momma some food, Mr. Butterfield," she announced.

"Not we, Miss Blair—you. She's your problem from here on. I came to get a hammer for one of the workmen upstairs and he's waiting for it."

After he had left, Connie stood looking down at the mother cat, settling herself among her babies. Poor soul, where had she come from?

" 'Pussycat, pussycat, where have you been?' "

The cat stared up, puzzled and pleading.

". . . to London, to see the Queen!' " Connie drew in a sharp breath as she said it to herself.

The Queen. The Queens! Along with the cats, had they, too, found refuge on the smoke shelf? Were they, right now, hidden in the gloom of a sooty corner where Mr. Butterfield's flashlight had failed to penetrate?

Her interest in the figurines rekindled, Connie started quickly for the fireplace. But, as she glanced again at the cat's quizzical eyes, humanity got the better of curiosity.

Lance always brought milk with his lunch. First she'd find Lance, beg some milk, and feed the cats. Then she'd investigate the smoke shelf!

CHAPTER 7

Suspicious Soot

"KITTENS? On the smoke shelf in the chimney?"

"Yes. And, Lance, would you do a good deed for the day for the S.P.C.A.?" Connie asked.

"Depends on the deed," Lance replied warily.

"Fill this with milk for the poor mother." She extended a cracked saucer she had found in the supply room.

Lance took the saucer. "Creeps," he said, obviously relieved, "I thought you were going to ask me to drown them! Sure I'll fill it," he offered obligingly. "The milk's in a bag with my sandwiches."

He went out of the living room where he had been taking pictures of the mantel, and rummaged among the coats on the bench in the hall.

"Here it is," he called, waving the bottle at

71

Connie. "Come on, we'll take her the whole pint. She may want seconds."

"Oh, Lance, don't you bother coming," Connie demurred. She had intended giving the cat the milk, making a hasty trip up the chimney, and then getting back to work. If Lance tagged along, he'd spoil her plan.

But Lance was insistent. Also, he'd been to the barber, Connie noticed, and apparently the tonsorial treatment had given him a lift. He was unusually jovial.

"I like kittens. I'd like to see these," he announced, leading the way to the supply room.

While Lance poured the milk, Connie lifted the mother cat out of the carton and placed her on the floor beside the saucer. She gave Connie a grateful look and then attacked the milk with vigor. "Heavens, she's certainly going at it!" Connie exclaimed.

"Yes," Lance agreed, "but milk's just hush-puppy stuff—I should say hush-pussy in this case. She needs real nourishment. During lunch hour I'll buy her some cans of cat food and raw hamburger."

"My, Lance"—Connie chuckled—"you really are going all-out in the cause of the felines."

Lance laughed. "Oh, well, I feel expansive today, Connie. My girl told me if I spruced up my appearance, maybe she'd accept me. So I got me a haircut and a new suit—and last night she did."

"Why, Lance, that's wonderful. Congratulations!"

Although, today, Lance was wearing the gray suit he usually wore to work, Connie noticed that it had been freshly cleaned and pressed. Lance looked nice. "When's the wedding?" she asked.

"In the spring, provided I get the wherewithal. But to get back to the kittens, are you positive Butterfield found the entire litter?"

"You mean one may have been overlooked? I hadn't thought of that, Lance. I'll see."

It was a perfect excuse to go back up the chimney. Connie stood up quickly and picked up the flashlight.

"I'll go," Lance offered. "I'm taller and—"

"You're cleaner, too," Connie reminded him hastily as she mounted the nail keg that was still standing on the hearth. Using the crane pin Mr. Butterfield had used for support, she boosted herself up and secured her elbows on the smoke shelf. Then she turned on the light.

"See any more?' Lance asked, and from the sound of his voice, Connie could tell that he was over by the cat carton.

"No."

A quick survey of the ledge told her that it was disappointingly bare of both kittens and *objets d'art*.

"There are just marks in the soot where they were and marks from my elbows and Mr. Butterfield's and—"

She broke off her report with a startled gasp. There were other marks, too—exciting marks. In the far corner to the right of where the mother cat had nursed her family, Connie's light revealed six identical circles, so distinct that they seemed engraved in the soot. Six circles about four inches in diameter, in twin rows of three each. And Earle Filmore had said the Queens stood on round, hollow pedestals about four inches in diameter . . .

"And what?" Lance prompted.

Connie heard his footsteps approaching the hearth. Because of his height, Lance would need only to step on the nail keg to be on eye level with the ledge. Of course the circles might convey nothing to him because he had come on the job at the Calder mansion about the same time as Connie, and that was after Drake had finished his search and the excitement over the figurines had waned. Very possibly Lance had never heard of them. But Connie decided she couldn't take that chance. The circles in the soot demanded a great deal of serious thought on her part before she let anyone else know about them.

"Don't walk into the fireplace, Lance," she warned. "You'll get crummy."

Then, with one more hasty glance at the far corner of the ledge, she extinguished her light, kicked her foot free of the crane pin, and dropped to the ground with a thud.

Lance fell back a pace from the hearth like a man suddenly confronted by a blast of hot air from an open furnace door.

"Brother!" he exclaimed. "The Blond Avalanche!"

The light revealed six identical circles

"See!" Connie laughed, confronting him with her sooty elbows and soiled smock. "Your nice gray suit would now be charcoal if you had joined me."

"But you gasped. I thought you'd made a find up there."

"What kind of find?" Connie countered. The gasp had been a giveaway, but she was satisfied that her ruse to keep him out of the chimney had worked.

Lance shrugged. "An antique Grecian urn, maybe. Or crown jewels."

Crown jewels! Connie smiled to herself. Unwittingly, Lance had mouthed a cliché that in this instance had particular significance. Crowns and Queens.

"The ledge was bare, Lance," she said truthfully as she walked over to a shelf and gathered together her art materials. She could fill her water pan in the washroom when she tidied up.

"I'll give Mom seconds on milk," Lance told her. "If anyone asks for me at the house, I'll be along directly."

The cherry print in the hall had proved stubborn and needed more soaking before it could be peeled off. Meanwhile, Connie was taking the opportunity to record another item for Sansom Paint and Paper Company's new line—the colors of the old woodwork paints. They had been prepared for her in much the same manner as the wallpaper, on a horizontal strip of the chair rail in the dining room.

Each successive coat of paint had been removed by careful dry scraping, presenting a pattern that was something of a cross between a paint manufacturer's color chart and a checkerboard that had been stretched out into a continuous row of squares.

Reproducing the exact colors was tedious, but required no imagination. For that, Connie was thankful because her brain was whirling with the discovery of the circles. Certainly, beyond any reasonable doubt, they had been left by the six figurines, which meant that the Queens, until recently, to judge from the sharpness of the outlines, had been standing on the smoke shelf.

Connie now had something to dig her teeth into—a clue that the figurines had been hidden as Maryanne insisted and not simply given away.

However, to suppose that an old lady seventy-nine had climbed up into the chimney with them in tow, even with the aid of a stepladder, was illogical. In all probability Miss Calder had appointed an agent to do it for her—someone she trusted.

Hardly Nellie, Connie decided, for Nellie was old, too—and frail, the policeman had described her. Two elderly women scrambling around the old fireplace just didn't add up. But Drake, faithful employee of the Calder Insurance Company and avowed friend of the family, might have been a natural selection. He stopped in frequently to see her, he had told Connie.

But Drake had stated definitely that no one,

except Nellie, had known they were missing from the mantle until after Miss Calder died. So, unless he wasn't telling the truth—

Her thoughts were interrupted as a color more difficult than the others claimed her attention, a pale blue green that she imagined contained gray, but which, when mixed, was off key. Selecting a tube of lampblack from her box, she substituted it for gray. But it, too, failed to give the elusive shade of the paint. Wiping her palette clean, she started afresh, putting a scant brushful of yellow ocher in with the blue green, all the while blaming herself for her inability to concentrate on matching the shade.

By noon, word of the kittens had spread and there was a general exodus to the supply room. "Aren't you coming to see them again, Miss Blair?" Mr. Butterfield asked, stopping by her chair on one of his interminable trips in and out of the building.

Connie shook her head. "No. I've just caught the combination for this color and I want to get it down on paper." The yellow ocher had done the trick, but it had needed the lampblack after all, a mere touch of it.

"But the kittens are your responsibility, you know."

"Mine?"

Mr. Butterfield grinned and Connie was aware once more of his neglected teeth. "Sure, you'll have to take them home tonight. Drake will be here later and he won't let them stay."

Connie had never given this predicament a thought, but Mr. Butterfield had correctly evaluated the situation. Drake would never let the kittens stay, not even one night.

"But I can't take them, Mr. Butterfield!" she exclaimed, looking up at him, her big eyes filled with concern. "There's a firm rule at my aunt's apartment house—no animals!"

"Same holds true where I live. At least"—his smile broadened and he rubbed his chin—"that's the rule. They don't count domesticated vermin."

"Where do you live?"

"Little room, few blocks away." He thumbed over his shoulder toward the river.

Putting down her palette regretfully, Connie stood up. "All right. I'll come. I'd better talk to Lance."

He was in the supply room, feeding the cat canned food in the broken dish on the floor. A half-dozen workmen were grouped around the kittens, watching the tiny creatures squirming in their carton. Most people are kind, Connie thought to herself, and these poor little waifs needed kindness. Most pertinently, they needed a home.

"Lance," she asked without a preamble, "where do you live? I mean, could you take the kittens home?"

Lance straightened and scratched his head meditatively. "My father's dead. I live in an apartment about two feet square with my mother.

She works. She takes a lot from me, but I doubt if it includes kittens. Can't you take them, Connie?"

"No. I share an apartment uptown with my aunt Bet, and they don't allow animals."

If only she were in Meadowbrook, Connie wished. Despite Ruggles, there was always room for a stray at the Blairs', temporarily, anyway, until other arrangements could be made.

"What's wrong with parking them here until they're bigger?" one of the men suggested. "Then we can give them away one by one."

"Sure, I'll take one for my kids," a red-haired carpenter offered. "After they're old enough to lap. That black job with the white collar, say."

"But Mr. Drake will never allow it," Connie countered, turning to Lance for support. "You know that, Lance."

"Oh, so that's what's behind all this. Skip it, Connie," Lance said lightly. "I'll settle Andy."

Andy? Of course, Andrew Drake. Connie had almost forgotten he had a first name and it sounded peculiar to hear Lance use it. Except for Mr. Calder, everyone else called him simply Drake.

"Incidentally, Connie," Lance said, dumping the remainder of the can of cat food into the saucer for the cat, "several days ago you asked me for some shots of the hardware on the hall door for your sister. I finally remembered to bring them." He slipped his hand into his breast pocket and extracted the prints.

"Oh, thank you, Lance." As he handed her the photographs, Connie noticed a long smudge of soot on the inner side of his coat sleeve.

Had Lance been up the chimney? Had he seen the circles? Oh, that was plain silly, she thought. All men were interested in construction. Lance undoubtedly had bent down and looked up the fireplace to see how it was built and somehow his sleeve had brushed against the smoke-covered stones.

All afternoon while Connie worked she listened expectantly for the arrival of Mr. Calder. As owner of the property and nominal head of the family, he should be informed of her discovery as soon as possible.

She listened, too, for Drake's voice. It would be interesting, indeed, to watch his reaction when he learned she had been up the chimney.

But neither Calder nor Drake appeared and toward the end of the day she heard two of the workmen talking in the next room:

"Drake called. He won't be down until after five."

"How about the kittens?"

"That photographer fellow is going to leave him a note. Drake said Calder won't be down at all. He's home with a cold."

Connie went directly to the telephone closet under the stairs. This was Friday and what she had to tell Mr. Calder could not wait over the week end. But she couldn't risk saying much over the telephone because the closet door was warped and refused to shut by two inches. It would be best to make an appointment to see him.

A card with his office and home number was tacked on the back of the door. Connie dialed the suburban number and was connected immediately with Mr. Calder himself. Fortunately, as soon as he heard her voice, he asked if she had discovered anything interesting about the figurines and from Connie's end of the wire all she had to say was "yes." It was his suggestion that she come out to his house in Gwynedd and discuss it.

After she had talked to Mr. Calder, she called her aunt at Campion's. "I won't be home for dinner, dear. Something has come up."

"Something about the latest mystery?" Aunt Bet wanted to know in a voice in which Connie detected a trace of worry.

"Yes . . . I found—" she started to whisper the words "a clue" when she saw Mr. Butterfield in the hall—"a litter of kittens in an old fireplace," she ended brightly.

But as she replaced the phone in its cradle she saw in her mind's eye, not the kittens, but the telltale circles in the soot. If, as the marks indicated, the Queens had huddled in the gloom of the chimney not too many weeks ago, where did their ruby crowns rest now? Whose hands had put them on the smoke shelf and whose hands had reached up to remove them?

CHAPTER 8
The Clue Disappears

CONNIE stepped off the Chestnut Hill local at the end of the line, just as a black-and-white station wagon, long enough to double as a bus, pulled into a lighted parking space beside the platform. Even before it came to a full stop, two blond girls about ten, dressed in identical tan car coats, popped out and dashed up to Connie.

"Are you Miss Blair?" they asked in unison. "We're the Calder twins. Daddy said you were coming for dinner."

Connie smiled. "Well, yes. He was very gracious to ask me. We have some personal matters to discuss."

"We know. It's about the little statues. Do you like oyster stew?"

83

"Why, surely. I love it."

"That's good, because that's what we're having," the twin who had taken her right arm announced. The other clung to her left arm, and, together, they propelled her toward the automobile. "We always have it when Mommy's away because she hates it, and she's away now visiting our sister who's married and just had a baby. Here, you sit with Enid. I'll sit with Jeff. My name's Edie."

Jeff was the chauffeur. He touched his cap respectfully as Connie got in the middle seat followed by Enid.

"You work at Great-Aunt Carrie's house, don't you?" Enid asked, and then promptly answered herself. "Yes, Daddy told us all about you. You're an artist. Do you know our cousin? He works there, too."

"Your cousin?"

"Uh-huh. Lance. Lance Hurley."

"Why, yes, I know Lance. But I didn't know you were related."

"We are . . . sort of. I mean"—Enid clarified the relationship—"Daddy and Lance's mother were first cousins. Daddy is Lance's cousin once-removed and we're his second cousins."

"Oh."

That explained Lance's control over Mr. Drake concerning the kittens. It also accounted for Drake's sudden deferential turn-about-face when Lance called him down at the scene of

Happy's fire. If Lance had Calder blood, then he was someone to be respected by Andrew Drake. But if that were so—

"Your cousin told me he'd rarely seen your great-aunt, girls. How's that?"

"Well, you see, Great-Aunt Carrie didn't approve of Lance's father and—" Enid began, but was interrupted by her sister leaning over the front seat.

"Enid! It's not polite to talk about family skeletons!"

"Shut my mouth! Edie's right, Miss Blair. I'm sorry."

Connie was sorry, too, for a different reason. But she respected the twins' reticence. "Have you ever seen the figurines?" she asked lightly.

"Yes, indeed," Edie answered. "Once a year all the cousins went to Fifth Street for dinner— and Mr. and Mrs. Drake, too. All the cousins except the Hurleys, that is."

"Now who's talking about skeletons!" Enid chided.

They were passing along what appeared to be the main street of a small town, where the lighted shops displayed smart evening dresses, sports attire, and sporting equipment. Connie felt it appropriate to change the subject.

"Is this Chestnut Hill? It looks a little like Williamsburg," she remarked, noting the small-paned windows and a tiny, one-story bakery that reminded her so much of the wigmaker's establishment in Williamsburg.

"It's very old and it's been restored," Enid told her. "Some of the places aren't really old, though, so they built on old fronts. Look up and you can see."

Connie obeyed and was amazed at the conglomerate architecture on the second-floor fronts of the buildings. Mid-Victorian mingled with Early American, and Twentieth Century merged with Mid-Victorian.

"We live about five miles from here on a farm. Daddy told you to come to The Hill instead of Gwynedd station because it's a shorter train ride from town and Jeff had to pick up Nellie, anyway. She's spending the night with our cook and doing our mending."

"Oh. And where do we pick up Nellie?" Meeting Nellie was something Connie had not hoped for.

"Up the Pike a way," the twins said, again in unison.

As the car turned off the main street and started down a long, tree-lined hill, Connie read a sign: *Bethlehem Pike*. They rode in silence for about two miles and then stopped in front of a small stucco cottage that seemed to rise directly out of the street. The door to the cottage was not more than a couple of feet from them.

"My goodness"—Connie laughed—"this is really curb service."

"It sat farther back before the road was widened," Enid explained. "But there's a nice garden in the rear. That's why Nellie rented it."

"And because it was cheap," Edie supplied. "Nellie has her social security and the money Great-Aunt Carrie left her, and what Daddy helps out with, but she's not—well, rich, exactly."

Connie smiled to herself. A few minutes with the Calder twins and you had a complete dossier on the family.

Apparently Nellie expected them, for she came out from the cottage promptly, a thin, slightly stooped woman in a simple black coat and hat. As she got into the seat behind Connie, Enid made the introductions. "Miss Blair, this is Nellie. Nellie, Miss Blair is painting things at Great-Aunt Carrie's."

"And enjoying walking in your pretty garden, Nellie," Connie complimented her graciously.

"Oh, thank you, Miss Blair. I hope you'll see it this spring, after Mr. Calder has it tidied up. There are some new bulbs in, special double tulips from Holland."

"Yes, Mike told me. He's keeping an eye on the garden for you, Nellie."

"He is?" Nellie sounded genuinely pleased. "Well, bless his dear Irish heart."

"Miss Blair is coming to see Daddy about the little statues. Have you found them, Miss Blair?" Edie wanted to know, rolling down the front window at her elbow as far as it would go.

Connie was glad for the open window. The station wagon was getting stuffy. She breathed in the cool air gratefully, enjoying the good country smells of the farm land through which they were driving. It gave her time to consider how to answer Edie.

"No, I didn't find them," she said finally, truthfully.

"Mercy, I wish somebody would!" Nellie's voice from behind was unexpectedly vehement. "Such a fuss as is going on."

Connie turned around. "Oh, don't you think Miss Calder gave them away like the other things, Nellie?"

"No! But why didn't she tell someone what she did with them? Still," Nellie added, sighing, "maybe she meant to. But she passed away too soon. There's always so much time until suddenly it's too late."

Connie wanted to ask Nellie more, but as they started along a private lane, further conversation was interrupted by the arrival of a tremendous dog running alongside the car, barking wildly.

"It's Byrne!" Edie cried out. "Oh, Enid, we forgot to take him to the station and he's furious."

Jeff stopped the car and Edie admitted a highly excited red setter whom she tried in vain to confine to the front seat. But Byrne scrambled back and onto both Connie's and Enid's laps. If he had been furious, his demeanor had certainly changed. He pawed at them with uncontrollable joy and his tail banged with gusto.

"Grab him, Enid!" Nellie commanded. "He'll have Miss Blair a wreck."

Enid yanked at the setter until she had all of

him on her lap. "He's just a poor mixed-up pooch," she said fondly, cuddling him tightly in her arms. "We have other pets, too, Miss Blair—horses and cows and cats. We had a rabbit until yesterday, but he died."

"He's in a tin box waiting to be buried," Edie explained. "Only Jeff can't dig a grave because the ground's still too frozen underneath."

"I'll dig it over the week end if I have to use a pick," Jeff broke in. "The frost can't be too far down this early in the winter. Now you two stop worrying."

Connie sat listening idly, not much interested in the disposal of the dead rabbit, unaware that its delayed burial would be of special significance to her later.

As the car rolled to a stop, Mr. Calder himself met them at the door. Nellie remained inside and rode around to the rear with Jeff.

"Good evening, Miss Blair," Mr. Calder welcomed her. "I certainly appreciate your making this trip out here. Now, girls, you take Miss Blair in tow. She may want to freshen up a bit."

They trooped into a low-ceilinged hallway, filled with the pleasant warmth of home. Edie took Connie's coat and hung it in the side closet.

"Come with me," Enid squealed, taking Connie by the hand and leading her up a wide oak stairway.

Connie noticed the lovely details of the house in spite of the twins' constant chatter. At the first stair landing was a broad window seat padded with gold brocade and set into an enormous leaded-glass window. At the top of the stairs, she was pulled along the hallway to a charming chintzy bedroom. Just like something from an old English storybook, Connie thought.

"This is our room," the twins chorused. "The bathroom's there if you want to wash. We'll wait here."

Connie freshened up quickly and rejoined the twins. Although she had sensed the quiet but luxurious comfort of this obviously big house, she was even more impressed when they entered the living room. It was all the pictures rolled into one she had ever visioned of comfortable country living.

It rose two full stories to a cathedral ceiling with massive exposed beams. Its size seemed endless, but, for all that, it had a coziness emphasized by the thick-piled carpet and the fire roaring in the huge carved stone fireplace.

"Well," Mr. Calder announced when they were seated before the fire, "I'll bet I'm the only man in the valley surrounded by three beautiful blondes."

Connie had been apprehensive lest the Calders might dress for dinner, but, for all the luxury, life in the house seemed casual. Mr. Calder had on a gray tweed sports jacket. Except for the gold chain Connie was wearing, which seemed fitting since she was older, her camel-colored sweater and skirt were in perfect accord with the twins' brown outfits.

They rounded out a picture of the perfect gentleman-farmer's family.

"But I want this clearly understood," Mr. Calder went on, addressing his daughters. "There's to be no mention of Aunt Carrie's figurines among the four of us. Miss Blair and I will discuss them later." Then he turned to Connie. "They read too many mysteries. They're mystery mad. They'd make a mystery out of Byrne if he didn't have the good dog sense not to let them."

The setter had calmed down and was stretched in front of the fire. At mention of his name, his tail thumped twice against the rug. And, as if the tail-thumping had been the signal she'd been waiting for, the maid announced dinner.

The creamy oyster stew, accompanied by a delicious salad and plenty of Trenton crackers, was served in large bowls that Connie wished her mother could have seen. For years Mrs. Blair had bemoaned the fact that it was no longer possible to buy large soup bowls, unless you were lucky enough to run across them in an antique shop.

"The girls selected the menu tonight," Mr. Calder explained, seeming to apologize for such plain fare. "Even the dessert."

"And that's the best part," Edie said with a grin.

Table talk centered around the girls' school, the prowess of the hockey team which recently had won the interpreparatory championship, and at the ability Byrne had displayed during the November hunting season.

"This was his first year in the field," Mr. Calder said proudly as the maid brought in the dessert.

It was a strawberry ice-cream cake, topped with whipped cream. Calorie-wise it was ghastly; gastronomically, Connie found it divine.

"We'll have coffee in the library, Miss Blair," Mr. Calder said after they had finished.

"And we'll be banished to do our lessons," Edie said dolefully. " 'By now, Miss Blair. It was fun meeting you."

"Good night, Edie. Good night, Enid."

"Good night, Miss Blair. And if you get a clue to the little statues"—Enid winked, giving her father a mischievous glance—"let us in on it."

"Maryanne has them all steamed up over those blasted figurines," Mr. Calder sighed as the twins started upstairs. "But now, Miss Blair, tell me your news."

Over coffee Connie related her discovery of the circles on the smoke shelf. Mr. Calder showed intense interest mingled with surprise.

"Well, well, well. So apparently Aunt Carrie did hide them after all. Well, well," he repeated, and then his expression changed. "But that's not possible, Miss Blair. She was badly crippled with arthritis. Aunt Carrie could never have negotiated a trip up the chimney."

"No, it stands to reason she must have had someone do it for her."

Mr. Calder nodded. "Yes, that theory holds water. But who? And why don't they speak up?"

Connie laid her coffee cup on the table in front of her. "It's conceivable they are ignorant of the present situation."

"I suppose it is. But where are the figurines? They're certainly missing. And it's highly unlikely a sneak thief would have come across them in an absurd place like the smoke shelf."

"I think so, too," Connie agreed. "It does seem whoever removed them must have known they were there."

Mr. Calder put his cup on the table beside Connie's. "Yes, it would seem so," he said thoughtfully. "Even Andy didn't find them . . . unless, of course, they had been taken away before he made his search."

"That's perfectly possible," Connie allowed honestly. "I have no idea when they were taken away, naturally—I just feel it wasn't as far back as early summer. The marks are too distinct. They're not filled in with dust or dirt."

Mr. Calder threw his hands up in despair. "Oh, rats," he exclaimed, "I give up! Why couldn't she have put them in a bank vault like any normal person! But that was Aunt Carrie for you—self-sufficient unto herself. And look at all the trouble she's causing! The only amusing part of the whole mixed-up business is Andy—he's the watchdog of the family. It will kill him when he learns he missed what you discovered."

He rose suddenly. "But since you did make the discovery in the chimney, I'll have to take some action for Maryanne's sake. But before I call on the police, I want to see those circles for myself so that I can substantiate your clue. I'll drive you home, Miss Blair, then go down to Fifth Street."

"But you're not well, Mr. Calder . . ."

"I'm better. Fruit juices are all very fine, but there's nothing like a square meal to knock a cold. Or maybe"—he grinned boyishly—"it was that frightful concoction of a dessert that did it."

For the first fifteen minutes of the ride to town Mr. Calder said very little and nothing about the mystery, although Connie knew he was thinking about it, for he had the same worried expression she remembered from the day he had told her he was expecting the visitor who turned out to be Maryanne Jessup.

Connie was glad to relax in silence. She was unusually tired, and the lights from the oncoming stream of traffic on the River Drive acted as a soporific. She wondered if, as her mother would say, she was "coming down with something."

The East Drive was closed for repairs at the Falls Bridge and they were forced to detour. As they crossed the Schuylkill River, Mr. Calder began to speak, almost as though he were talking to himself, "I'm really afraid to start an investigation. We've had so much wrangling in the family lately, and now, to have the police breathing down all our necks . . . they'll be bound to consider the element of theft. Maybe they'll figure it's an inside job. Why, I don't know, since none of us needs money . . . except Lance Hurley.

But Lance has nothing to do with it, I'd stake my life on that! Besides, he'd never do anything that would hurt Maryanne. She was too good to him and his mother. He's moody like his father, but he's honest. Still, the police may think differently. They may pounce on him because of his background—"

"Mr. Calder!" Connie interrupted, pointing to her right. "The detour turns here, up past the zoo."

Mr. Calder had become so engrossed in his problems that he had failed to see the sign. He was headed straight along, toward more construction work.

"That's typical of Philadelphia," he snapped impatiently as he swerved the car. "Tear up all the roads at the same time!"

His display of temper was not characteristic of him, Connie knew, and was brought about solely by worry.

"Don't be upset about the figurines," she remonstrated gently. "There's no proof they've been stolen. The police may locate them without any fuss whatsoever."

"That's kind of you to say, Miss Blair," he acknowledged gratefully, after a moment in which he had obviously collected himself. "I did rather talk myself into a storm, didn't I? And please forget what I said about Lance. I certainly don't want to leave you with any false impressions. Lance is a grand person and a good photographer. I was happy to be able to throw the job with Reid and Renshaw for the Sansom Company his way. . . . You did tell me the address of your apartment before we left Gwynedd, but now I must confess I've forgotten it."

Connie repeated it and again they lapsed into silence. As they pulled up before the apartment, Mr. Calder said seriously: "Miss Blair, I'm trying to piece together some plan of procedure. I may call in a private detective instead of the police. But until I do either, I'm convinced no one in the family, except Maryanne, should know about your find. Can I depend on you to keep it a secret?"

"Of course, Mr. Calder," Connie agreed. But she smiled inwardly—keeping things secret was getting to be a game.

As she opened the apartment door, she saw a note stuck in the ivy planter in the foyer which she and Aunt Bet used for interfamily communications.

"Am at Earle F's playing bridge," it read. *"Don't wait up."*

Connie was sorry that her aunt was out. She didn't feel at all well and could stand a little mothering from someone older. As it was, she went to the medicine cabinet, found the old family grippe capsules, and took two as directed. Then she undressed and crawled into bed, hoping that she'd feel better by morning.

About now, she figured drowsily before she fell asleep, Mr. Calder must be halfway up the chimney.

The incessant jingle of the telephone awakened her. Sleepily she stumbled into the living room and lifted the instrument.

"Hello."

"Miss Blair?"

"Yes."

"Sorry to disturb you. Montgomery Calder. There are no marks of circles on the smoke shelf. All I could find was a lot of soot all smudged up—most likely by your cat family."

"Oh, no, Mr. Calder!" Connie exclaimed. "Oh, no! Did you look in the right-hand corner?"

"Most particularly. In fact, the soot isn't even smudged there—it's smooth as silk. You know, Miss Blair, people often think they see things when actually—reflected light sometimes—"

He let the insinuation hang in mid-air and Connie didn't argue with him. Mr. Calder had found what he wanted to find, no proof that there was any mystery in connection with the missing figurines. Any explanation Connie might make he'd catalogue as pure fantasy.

She said good-by and went back to bed completely stunned. Someone had obliterated the circles! If they had still been there, Mr. Calder couldn't have failed to see them—they were far, far too distinct.

Someone had purposely erased the clue that testified the Queens had been hidden and not merely given away!

CHAPTER 9

A Talk with Maryanne

"No FEVER!" Elizabeth Easton announced, returning the thermometer to the bedside table.

"I feel almost normal," Connie admitted, lying back against the pillow. Her throat was decidedly better. Only a terrific laziness warned her that there might still be a bug inside her. "All I've got now is lead legs."

"Lead legs?"

"Yes . . . full of lead instead of blood and bones and muscles."

"Well, since this is Saturday, you stay right where you are, dear. I'll bring you a glass of orange juice before I leave."

Saturdays were workdays in the retail clothing business and Aunt Bet was already dressed for her job. Connie did not like the prospect of being left alone. To be mothered was very pleasant. She stretched and rolled languidly on her side, enjoying the remaining short time of tender nursing care. Later, she'd think about the puzzling situation at the old house.

"I almost forgot." Aunt Bet paused at the door. "Your young man, Happy Wallace, called while you were out last night. He wants you to go to a tea dance this afternoon at his fraternity house. But I guess—"

Connie bounded out of her lethargy as though she had been jet-propelled. She sat up, threw off the covers, and said brightly:

"Mr. Calder says that solid food is the best remedy for a cold. I'm going to have a big breakfast . . . bacon and eggs and those rolls I saw in the breadbox . . . heated . . . and coffee . . ."

Aunt Bet chuckled. "If that's what you want, I'm going to stop worrying about you. And while you're eating like a little pig, you can brief me on the events at Fifth Street. I'm behind schedule. You were sound asleep when I came in last night."

Whenever Connie promised to keep a secret, she crossed her fingers about Aunt Bet. Aunt Bet was the confidante to whom she told everything. And so, in the breakfast alcove, after a detailed account of the clue in the chimney, the trip to Gwynedd, and Mr. Calder's subsequent telephone call, she said reflectively:

"Whoever obliterated the circles, knew about the kittens being rescued—and the only people who knew about the kittens were the people in the building."

Mr. Drake hadn't been there, but Lance had left him a note. Connie wondered if the note mentioned where the kittens had been found.

"Is there any chance some outsider might have visited the supply room before Mr. Calder?" Aunt Bet asked.

"I doubt it. Mr. Butterfield was locking up when I left."

"Well," Miss Easton said as she started toward the foyer, "one thing is positive. Whoever did it was determined that the clue that the Queens had been hidden—and where—shouldn't be proved."

"Yes, that's for sure," Connie sighed. "Mr. Calder acted as though I dreamed it up. And now," she announced with sudden spirit, buttering a roll, "I'm as determined as the culprit. I'm going to prove those circles were real!"

Aunt Bet's face clouded. "I wish you wouldn't, dear. I'm afraid you're running into danger. Still, I don't suppose my wishing will alter your decision." She shrugged resignedly as she took a short Persian lamb jacket from the closet. Her next words were spoken more lightly. "Let's forget it for the nonce and be feminine. What are you wearing to the dance?"

"My green with the silver buttons. Isn't that all right?" Connie asked tentatively when her aunt failed to respond immediately. "I can't afford a new one so near Christmas."

"Well, I can. And I abhor that green. It doesn't

even fit properly. Would you like your Christmas present early?"

"You mean . . ." Connie's eyes opened wide with anticipation.

"I mean, we just received a shipment of darling silks. Stop by Campion's today if you're well enough and charge one to me."

Whether it was the prospect of a new dress, the cold capsules she'd taken the night before, or the big breakfast, Connie didn't know, but by ten o'clock she felt healthy as ever. She called Happy at the drafting-room number he had left with Aunt Bet and accepted his invitation. His design problem was due at five, he told her, and he'd stop by for her after he had shaved and cleaned up.

Connie dressed quickly and went to Campion's. Purposely, she wore no hat, for hats, to her, were mentally constricting and her mind needed figurative airing. For the next couple of hours she vowed to forget about statuettes of queens, circles in the soot, suspects—everything connected with the mystery. "Clear your perspective, Connie," she told herself. "Then tackle the situation objectively."

In the dress department, she selected a champagne-colored sheath. Aunt Bet had been correct, the new shipment of silks was darling, and it was quite a problem to make a choice. But the sheath, she felt, "did things" for her slim figure.

"That color is perfect for blondes," the stout woman who was waiting on her commented, admiring Connie's reflection in the dressing-room mirror.

"Is it too long?" Connie asked, turning around slowly.

"A bit, but the store's not promising any alternations for a week or more."

"Oh, well, if I can have a pin fitting, I'll hem it myself this afternoon."

After the fitting, Connie went to the main floor and bought a cardigan for Kit. The price tag was astronomical, but the sweater was the softest cashmere imaginable and, after all, Kit was her only sister.

"Do you want it gift wrapped?" the salesclerk asked.

Connie nodded. "Please."

"Miss Blair?"

Connie turned. For a moment she did not recognize the smart, black-suited woman standing next to her at the counter.

"I'm Maryanne Jessup, Montgomery Calder's cousin," the woman explained, noticing Connie's temporary confusion.

"Oh, of course. I met you at Fifth Street."

Where, except in Philadelphia, could a woman change her appearance so suddenly and so completely? One minute looking as though she belonged in a barn and the next in a fashion magazine.

"I'm surprised you remembered me," Connie added.

"I couldn't forget that hair," Mrs. Jessup replied, returning Connie's smile. "Besides, Mont and I were talking about you not an hour ago, Miss Blair. I'm so grateful that you discovered those marks in the old chimney. They prove I was right—that Aunt Carrie did save the figurines for me as she'd promised."

"I'm afraid Mr. Calder doesn't think so, even now," Connie said ruefully. "I'm sure he thinks it's some kind of hallucination."

"Montgomery is a realist, my dear. He's sure you and I—like his twins—are mystery mad. But I believe you. It's just a shame the cat family smudged up the soot before Montgomery looked up the chimney. If he'd seen the circles, he would have been forced to take some action."

Connie was a little startled at the mention of the cats smudging the circles until she realized that Maryanne didn't know the complete story and had simply surmised that the cats were responsible for Mr. Calder's not seeing the marks.

"However," Mrs. Jessup continued before Connie had a chance to acquaint her with the details, "you and I know there *is* a mystery concerning the present whereabouts of the figurines. But I agree with Montgomery"—her speech slowed and her face seemed troubled—"in not wanting to contact the police or a private detective agency. We have so little to go on and—and then there's Lance."

She paused and looked appealingly at Connie. "Miss Blair, Montgomery said you had quite a reputation for solving puzzles. Do you think if we two women got our heads together—I mean, have you a moment to talk?"

Connie gave up all intention of clearing her perspective on the mystery. It would be far more instructive to hear what Mrs. Jessup had to say. "Yes, I have time to talk, Mrs. Jessup."

Momentarily, they were interrupted by the salesclerk handing Connie her purchase. Tucking the gaily wrapped package under her arm, along with the box containing the dress, she followed Maryanne to a divan in the corner of the salesroom. They sat down and Connie laid her packages on the floor beside her. Maryanne unclasped the fur piece she was wearing over her suit and threw it across her lap.

"May I call you Connie?"

"I'd love you to." Connie liked the friendly gesture. Mrs. Jessup, although not pretty, had a gracious manner that lent her definite charm.

"Do you know about Lance?" she asked.

"No," Connie replied. "Mr. Calder mentioned him last night."

It didn't seem polite to admit that the twins had referred to the Hurleys as the family skeleton.

"Well," Mrs. Jessup began in a straightforward way that Connie admired, "Lance's father was in jail most of Lance's childhood, on an embezzlement charge. The poor youngster grew up under a frightful stigma. Every time anything was missing at school— Oh, you can imagine what the other children said."

Connie nodded. It was not a happy picture.

"Added to that, the Hurleys were impoverished. My cousin, Lance's mother, was an orphan and had money of her own, but she spent it all trying to clear her husband's name. Aunt Carrie, who had been her guardian, had opposed the match from the beginning. Well, to make a long story short, Lance and his mother had a good many bad years. I did what I could to help . . ."

She didn't enlarge, but Connie could well imagine the nice things a person of Maryanne's fine character would do for anyone in trouble.

"But Aunt Carrie made a real charity case out of their unfortunate plight," Maryanne continued. "She never visited them or had them to her house. But she sent them things—canned goods, clothes for Lance, dull, drab, and durable and always six sizes too big so that he wouldn't outgrow them in a hurry. But never a toy for the child, nor a pretty gift for his mother—nor a kind word."

She paused with a faraway look in her eyes as though recalling the past. Now Connie could easily understand Lance's low opinion of Miss Carrie Calder.

"Still," Maryanne sighed, "Aunt Carrie may not have intended to be mean, but with all her money . . . Anyway, the minute Lance was able, he flatly refused any more of what he termed 'Aunt Carrie's belittling benevolence.' I'm sorry he did that, otherwise she might have remembered him in her will.

"But to get back to the figurines," she said, snapping out of her reverie, "we did go to the police in one respect. We had them check—and they are still keeping check on—all the antique shops. But the Queens haven't turned up. Oh, I suppose I'm too optimistic in thinking they ever will.

"Anyhow, I'm glad about the circles. With all her faults, I was fond of Aunt Carrie, Connie, and I'm happy she didn't break her word."

"You mentioned that a minute ago, Mrs. Jessup," Connie said, thinking back to the beginning of their conversation, "about her promise. Just what did she promise?"

"Oh, yes, I didn't explain that, did I? Well, the day I sailed for abroad I had lunch with Aunt Carrie. She told me she had decided to give away some of her things. If I hadn't been on my way to New York to get my boat, she'd have given me the Queens then, but she promised me to find a safe place to store them out of Nellie's reach. She wasn't so much afraid of theft as she was that Nellie, who was getting feeble, might break them in dusting. But there's one thing I can't understand—" she broke off, meditating.

"What's that, Mrs. Jessup?"

"Aunt Carrie may have been eccentric, but she was also a very provident woman. She never would have overlooked the contingency of her death. Why didn't she leave instructions that the Queens be given to me if anything happened to her—"

"I think she did," Connie broke in quietly. "I think those instructions were disregarded."

"What?"

"Mrs. Jessup, there's something you don't know. It's about the cats. The cats didn't smudge up the circles on the smoke shelf. It was *after* the cat family was *out* of the chimney that I discovered the circles. Someone, some person, obliterated them."

"Obliterated?" Maryanne repeated in amazement. "You mean purposely?"

"Yes. Someone smoothed over the soot and erased the clue that proved the Queens had been hidden there."

The fur piece on Maryanne's lap slipped to the floor. She stared at it for a while before she leaned over and picked it up. Summing up in her mind the import of Connie's statement, she said slowly, "Then the Queens have been *stolen*. And undoubtedly by the same person who hid them."

"Yes," Connie said emphatically. "It's the obvious answer. Mrs. Jessup, have *you* any idea who it might be?"

Maryanne stood up and glanced at the clock over the divan. "No, not the slightest. And now I must rush to keep an appointment. But first, there's something I want clear. I've bored you with my chatter because, as I said, I hoped that if we two women got our heads together— Well, I hoped we might locate the figurines. But I've changed my mind." The pleasant camaraderie dropped from her voice and she sounded like a mother giving implicit directions to a small child. "This is one mystery I insist you stay out of!" Then, apparently feeling she had been overbearing, she added gently:

"I've been stupid, Connie. I didn't realize we were dealing with a criminal. Why, I'd never forgive myself if anything happened to you because of me. My figurines probably are a lost item, anyway—the thief is undoubtedly too clever to have left a trail." And, with a farewell smile, she walked off.

Sympathetically, Connie watched Maryanne's retreating back. Crime, especially if it were near home, so to speak, must be shocking to someone like Mrs. Jessup. But to Connie, solving crime was an old story and Maryanne's admonition to stay out of this mystery had fallen on deaf ears. Furthermore, Connie didn't agree that the Queens were a "lost item." If they had been disposed of successfully by surreptitious private sale, or to an unscrupulous dealer who might have smuggled them out of the country, the culprit wouldn't have gone to the trouble of obliterating the circles. So somewhere along the line he must have made a mistake of which he was well aware. He couldn't afford to let a clue stand that would reopen interest in the case. He was afraid of further investigation.

And suddenly, as she picked up her purchases and started out the store, Connie was conscious of an insatiable desire to see the Queens for herself.

CHAPTER 10

Connie Goes Over the Wall

CONNIE was glad she had worn her pearls. Everyone, she noticed, as she milled through the crowd on her way to the powder room, was quite dressed up. She must remember to tell Kit about this evening. To her knowledge, Kit had never been inside a fraternity house at a big university.

Handing the brown velvet coat she had borrowed from Aunt Bet to the maid in attendance, she gave one last look in the mirror over the dressing table. It was a mere squint, actually, since a dozen other girls were attempting the same thing. Then she joined Happy in the hall.

"I approve," Happy said. "You had your coat on when I picked you up. I didn't see the gown."

They went down three steps into the living room where the orchestra was set up near the fireplace at the far end. Because of Happy's design problem, they had been late in arriving and the party was in full swing. The floor was crowded, but Happy proved to be a good dancer, and adroitly avoided tangling with other couples.

"Hap, where are you from?" Connie asked. "Come to think of it, I don't know one thing about you."

"New York, originally. My family is living in Florida now on account of Dad's health. And if you're curious about how I can afford to belong to this house, Miss Nosy"—he grinned—"I'm a legacy. I mean, Dad was a Deke when he was in college. So it's a must for me even if I starve."

Connie felt as if her entire head was a transparent glass. How he could afford it was exactly what she had been wondering and it had been prying and none of her business. Quickly she steered the conversation into another channel.

"We found a litter of kittens on Fifth Street today."

"So I heard."

"You did? How?"

"I have my spies," he responded archly.

"Oh, applesauce. Aunt Bet told you on the 'phone last night. But, Hap, knowing about the kittens puts you on my list."

Happy's brown eyes twinkled. "Your list? Who are you, anyway, the Lord High Executioner? I sang that part when we gave *The Mikado* in prep school. 'The L.H.E. chopped off heads—' "

"Never mind," Connie interrupted. "I'm being a bore talking shop."

"Yes," Happy agreed, "you are. I asked a *girl* for a date, remember, not a private eye."

The dance ended all too soon. Small groups broke off to go other places. Several of Happy's fraternity brothers suggested that he and Connie join them, but he had other plans.

"Frankly, Connie," he told her apologetically, "I'm too bushed after that charette to mix with the crowd. There's a new place downtown. It's quiet and you can eat well. My invitation included dinner. Didn't your aunt tell you?"

"No, she didn't. But if she knows, then I won't have to call her. Happy, would it be out of our way to stop at the old house? I'm concerned about Momma cat."

"You mean maybe she hasn't been fed? Okay, we'll pick up some food at a delicatessen. Convenient of my roommate to be at Amherst with the basketball team, isn't it?"

Connie looked puzzled. "What's your roommate got to do with it?"

"He's supplying the taxi service. I've got the green convertible for the whole week end."

They got their coats and started for the parking lot behind the fraternity house.

"Will we need a flash, or is there a light in the supply room?" Connie queried.

"There's a hundred-watter. We rigged it temporarily. All you do is reach up and tighten the bulb. I can feel it in the dark."

On Sixth Street, a pre-Christmas office party was in progress in the Ledger Building. The top floor was a blaze of lights and sounds of music floated down into the Square from windows that had been opened for ventilation. Cars were parked bumper to bumper, even on Fifth. Happy drove down Chestnut Street to Fourth, where, near the corner, he found an empty spot.

"We can cut through the alley beside the garden," he said, gathering up the three cans of cat food he had thrown on the seat between them. "The key to the supply room is on a hook by the rear door."

As they approached the iron fence, they could see into the garden, dimly illuminated by the reflected light from the city street lamps. Individual objects were indiscernible and the shrubbery mingled with the shadows to form distorted masses of forbidding shape. The house itself, at first glance, was dark, and, lacking the usual hum of daytime activity, the mantle of age had slipped over it. It seemed lonely, deserted, a thing of the past.

But it wasn't deserted—not entirely.

"Hap, look," she whispered, subconsciously lowering her voice. "Isn't there a flashlight moving around in the supply room?"

"Why, so there is. Someone else must have remembered Ma." He said it lightly, but Connie felt his arm tighten and she knew his reaction was identical to hers. If someone were feeding the cat, why not turn on the hundred-watt bulb?

Happy motioned her to get behind him. "I'll sneak up and see who it is. You stay here."

"I'm going with you," Connie insisted.

"Okay, Connie Commando, *we'll* sneak up."

He was about to unlatch the gate when she intervened. "Wait! If we cross the garden, we may be spotted. Let's go through the house."

"That makes sense, if anything does." Happy, too, was whispering. "What are we doing this for, anyway?"

"I'll explain later." She realized that Happy was still in ignorance concerning the circles and the importance the supply room had assumed in the last thirty-six hours, but there was not time to tell him. "Happy, who has a key to the house?"

"Drake, Lance, Butterfield—Calder, natch— all of us who are likely to work odd hours."

"None of the general workmen?"

"No."

They hurried along the alley and reached the end of the fence where it connected with the house. Suddenly Happy gave Connie a shove ahead of him, past the side wall which would screen them from view of the supply room.

"The light just went out," he muttered under his breath. "If that means someone's leaving, and he goes out the garden gate—"

"We'll miss him if we go through the house," Connie supplied quickly. "You watch the gate. I'll watch the front door, just in case."

Freeing her arm, she raced along the pavement and stationed herself at the Fifth Street corner of the house, peering around the end of the building. If anyone came out and went south on the street, she might be able to identify the retreating back. But if the person came north on Fifth Street, her only chance of remaining unnoticed would be to flatten herself against the wall and hope he did not turn into the alley. There would be no time to dash back to the garden and hide in the shrubbery.

Happy's position at the other end of the house was like hers in reverse. From the garden, it would be a mere happenstance if he escaped being seen. Of course, if this person's mission were purely humanitarian—and that eliminated Mr. Drake so far as Connie was concerned—he'd just be amused by the whole episode. But there had been something terribly suspicious about that moving light.

No one came out the front door. Connie craned her neck until it cramped. No lights went on inside the house. Saturday night in this historical section of Philadelphia, with its lack of retail establishments, was normally quiet and now it was in a dinner-hour lull. No pedestrians passed and practically no traffic.

"See anyone?" Happy asked, tapping her on the shoulder.

Connie wheeled. "No. Did you?"

"Nope, but I thought I saw the light again. He still must be in there. Come on. We'll tiptoe through the hall and go out the back door. We'll be able to see from the porch if anyone's still there."

Happy unlocked the door, and due to their

respective knowledge of the house, they were able to thread their way through the hall without bumping into anything.

"The supply room key is gone," Happy announced in his hushed voice as Connie opened the door to the garden. "He must have it."

The prospect from the porch was disappointing. The supply room was totally dark, but Connie was sure the door was standing open. If anyone were inside he might easily have heard the creaking of the back door and switched off his light. Keeping close to the house, and with Happy a step behind her, Connie edged her way along the wall.

"Here, let me go first," Happy said close to her ear.

Before she could stop him, he brushed past her and, in his haste, tripped over her foot. Her shoe came off, and then, to her horror, she heard Happy go down with a thud and the cans of cat food clatter across the brick terrace.

Limping on one stockinged foot, Connie ran toward the supply room, through its open door, and hunted frantically over her head for the light bulb. After that warning racket, if she were to catch anyone red-handed, it would have to be quick. She could worry about Happy later.

She found the bulb sooner than she'd thought possible and tightened it into the socket. For a second she stood blinking under its glare. Then, as her eyes became accustomed to the sudden brilliance, she saw that she was alone except for the kittens and the mother cat who stared up at her from the box with large, surprised hazel eyes. And the saucer contained only a few leftover dried crumbs of food. Whoever had been in the supply room had not come to feed the cat.

On the workbench, written on a large piece of brown wrapping paper and weighted down with a screw driver, she saw Lance's note.

> *Andy:*
>
> *The newcomers in the corner were discovered up the chimney by Miss B and Butterfield. Don't disturb them— they're boarding.*
>
> L. H.

And, typically, as though it had been an office memo sent to him for his attention, Drake, with true business protocol, had added his own initials to show he had read the note.

So Drake, too, knew she had been up the chimney!

Hurrying back to the porch, she regained her shoe as Happy was rising on his hands and knees. "Nobody there," she panted, reaching out to help him. "Are you hurt?"

Before Happy could answer, the fence gate clanged. Simultaneously they both turned in the direction of the garden. From his half-crouched position, Happy toed off like a runner hearing the starting signal and sprinted away from her in pursuit of a hastily glimpsed figure disappearing down the alley. Pulling her skirt up to her knees to free her legs, Connie followed.

As she gained the alley, Happy was rounding the corner into Fourth Street. She was half a block behind him and no match for his speed. Negotiating the uneven bricks in her high heels was an exasperatingly slow process.

She made better time when she reached the smoother surface on Fourth Street, but now a whole block separated them. Only here, however, the light was a little better. Happy stopped short at the corner of the next intersection, and, seeming to have lost his quarry, looked left and right, silhouetted against the neon sign in a drugstore window. Suddenly, to her chagrin, he moved to the right and disappeared behind the buildings just as a figure darted from an alley farther down the street.

When Connie reached the corner, Happy was retracing his steps. "I goofed . . ." he breathed heavily.

"That way!" Connie pointed excitedly ahead of her. "That way, Hap!"

He was off again, and once more Connie could not keep the pace. She saw Happy cut diagonally across the street, but she had lost track of the figure who had darted from the alley. And, at that moment, she lost track of Happy.

She slowed to a fast walk. The night was unseasonably warm and she was as hot as if she had played a set of tennis under a midsummer sun. The farther she went, the more hopeless she considered the chase. The section she was in was residential, poorly illuminated and traversed by alleys and narrow, arched passages that led from the street to the gardens behind the row houses. With a good lead, anyone could evade a pursuer here.

She crossed the street as Happy had done and noticed that the area ahead on her left was unusually dark, devoid even of lighted windows. She hurried on and found out why. A church and brick wall surrounding the churchyard, which she judged to be an old cemetery, took up the entire block.

Her feet were killing her, so she rested a moment against the wall. It was pointless to start running after Happy again, up and down and in and out the maze of alleys. Still, she couldn't stay where she was. On her whole trek down Fourth Street, she had passed no one. Respectable as the church block might be, it was lonely, dark, and dismal, a perfect place for a holdup. Folding her clutch purse, she stuffed it into the pocket of her coat. Perhaps she'd better go back to the car and—

She spied Happy. He was sprinting up Fourth Street in her direction. But before he noticed her, he stopped, pulled himself to the top of the wall and leaped into the churchyard.

Connie stifled an impulse to call out to him. If Happy had a chance to corner his prey behind the wall, she must not give his presence away.

The wall was substantial, built on a footing that projected slightly about two feet above the sidewalk. Stepping up on the projection, Connie

Connie was pushed headlong into the churchyard

rested her hands on top of the wall and pulled herself up until she was leaning over the coping, the upper part of her body half inside the yard.

In the darkness beyond, she thought she could detect movement, imagined she could hear running footsteps, but she couldn't be sure. With every muscle taut, she listened intently. Yes, she did hear something, heavy breathing, just below her. But it seemed to come—

Suddenly rough hands gripped her ankles and her feet were torn from their teetering perch. Instinctively she tried to kick out, but the clutch was firm and, to her horror, she lost her balance and sprawled on her stomach across the coping. Her hands felt for a hold she couldn't find, a crevice to cling to, a momentary block against the impending disaster that made her throat constrict and her heart pump wildly.

Was she about to be pushed over the wall? And by whom? From her present position, even if it had been daylight, her assailant was hidden from her view by the shelter of the wall.

"Hap!" she managed to cry.

Again she tried to kick free, but the grip on her ankles only tightened as her feet were raised higher in the air and her body was shoved forward horizontally. Helpless, her clawing hands sliding over the coping as though it were slippery marble, Connie realized she was about to plunge headlong into the churchyard.

In one last moment of consciousness she thought frantically, "I may be killed!"

CHAPTER 11

The Elusive Quarry

CONNIE fought to open her eyes. Vaguely she heard Happy saying her name again and again—heard him calling to her from what seemed outer space. She could not answer. He was too far away.

"Connie!"

Now Happy was right beside her, kneeling on the ground, bending over her, cradling her head in one arm. In the dimness his outline was barely, but comfortingly, discernible.

"Good grief, are you all right?"

"I guess so. Where have I been?"

"Out like a light."

"Where am I now?" She couldn't orient herself.

"In a cemetery. But before you tell me how

121

you got here, are you hurt? The one thing I remember about my Boy Scout first-aid course is not to move a patient with broken bones."

"You mean I'll have to stay here all my life?"

"Connie, this is no time for jokes! Creeps, after you screamed I came back from the chase and charged around these tombstones like crazy. I wasn't even sure you were here until I practically tripped over you. It's black as the inside of a hat here."

"Oh, Hap, I didn't mean to be funny," Connie apologized. "I think I was just coming to." She moved her arms and legs experimentally. Except for a sprained ankle, they worked normally. "Somebody grabbed me by the feet, Hap, and pushed me over the wall. I remember now. I suppose it was so you'd come back and give up the chase. I landed here on the ground, but I must have banged my head on something hard."

Happy snapped on his cigarette lighter. "You conked it on some old guy's grave who died in 1798," he said, holding the lighter over the head-stone at her elbow. "Ghost causes concussion," he quipped, moving the lighter nearer Connie. "You haven't got one, a concussion, I mean, have you? There's a beautiful egg building up just where the part in your hair begins."

Sitting up, Connie felt the lump gingerly. It was sore, but, oddly, her head did not ache. Aunt Bet's coat, she saw, was covered with mud from the thawing ground, and the champagne sheath had a triangular rip in the skirt. Her Christmas present! Ruefully she said, "I'm 'the maiden all forlorn—' "

"And I'm 'the man all tattered and torn,' " Happy quoted, surveying the rip in his trousers where they had caught on the wall. "All that's missing is 'the cow with the crumpled horn—' "

" 'Who tossed the dog that worried the cat that killed the rat that ate the malt that lay in the house that Jack built,' " they finished in unison.

Repeating the homey little nursery rhyme made Connie feel better, less frightened. "But it was no cow with a crumpled horn that tossed me," she said.

"Seriously," Happy interjected, "you're a mess. Your face is scratched and dirty, and the place for you is home."

He killed the light and put the lighter back into his pocket.

"Oh, no, Happy, no! We must go back to Fifth Street! There's no telling what—"

Happy cut off her protest by slipping his arms under her body and picking her up. "Phooey on Fifth Street," he said.

Connie wriggled to free herself. "Hap, you can't carry me. I'm too heavy."

"That's what you say. And quit wiggling. One of the yens of my youth was to carry a damsel in distress. If you thwart me, I'll get a complex that will turn me into a juvenile delinquent."

"Post-juvenile," Connie corrected, smiling up at him. "There's an age limit of seventeen."

"You're a mighty gorgeous girl, even messed

up." Happy changed the subject, coming to a halt on the pavement outside the church grounds. "I just remembered," he mused. "We left a line out of that rhyme."

"We did?" Connie said lazily. "What line?"

"If I recall," he said fondly, " 'the man kissed the maiden all forlorn—' "

"Hey! What shenanigans is goin' on here?" a voice of authority boomed out in the quiet night, interrupting Happy's quotation. Over his shoulder, Connie saw Mike, Nellie's policeman friend, approaching like an avenging angel.

"Let me down—quick!" She giggled. "Or he'll think we're both delinquent."

"Why, if it isn't the artist lady!" Mike exclaimed. "She been hit by a car?"

He addressed himself to Happy, but Connie answered. "No, I fell over a wall."

"Fell over a wall?"

"It's a long story, Officer," Happy interposed, "and our first consideration is the young lady. I'm taking her home—but fast."

Mike obviously disapproved the situation. "I'm on night duty this week an' I don't much take to people gettin' battered up on my beat. You take her home, son, an' fast like you said, not like you're doin' . . .

"By the way," he added, "there was a light on in that outbuilding at the Calder place. Know anything about it?"

"Yes," Connie acknowledged, "I turned it on. I guess I forgot to turn it off." She didn't think it necessary to mention that she had left in such a great hurry.

"Well, I did it for you," Mike grumbled, but his rich brogue belied his gruffness. "Locked up, too. 'Tweren't nobody around an' there's tools aplenty in there just for the takin'. Oh, I fed that scrawny cat. Found food on the porch."

"Oh, Mike, how kind of you," Connie thanked him sincerely. "You do keep excellent tabs on this section, don't you?"

Mike's manner brightened. "I try," he beamed. "But say, miss, how come you called me by name?"

"Nellie told me. You remember Nellie, the little gardener?"

"An' sure I do. You ever see her?"

"Occasionally." It wasn't strictly the truth, but it would suffice.

"Give her my regards, will you, like a good girl? And remind her I'm still keepin' an eye on her shrubbery." And then, twirling his night stick and whistling a lilting Irish air, he continued on up the street.

"I buttered up the law on purpose, Hap," Connie explained when he was out of earshot. "He might come in handy someday."

"He might come in handy right now. Look, Connie, why not call Mike back? I won't leave you alone in this part of town again, but if you waited with Mike while I got the car, it'd save walking on that bum ankle."

"Heaven forbid!" Connie objected. "If my

wall-tossing friend is still in the neighborhood and noticed me talking with a policeman, I'd be murthered in me sleep." She laughed, mimicking Mike's brogue. If Happy got the car it would interfere with her plan, for she was determined to get back to the Calder mansion despite Happy's "phooey on Fifth Street."

Without making any immediate comment, Happy helped Connie down one curb and up another. Then he said thoughtfully, "To have tossed you over the wall, he must have doubled back. But I can't understand—"

"Who doubled back?"

"Lance."

"Lance?"

"Yes, Lance. The guy I was chasing."

"Oh, Happy, don't be absurd. I caught a glimpse of the man you were chasing. He was fairly short."

Happy shook his head emphatically. "You're wrong, Connie. He was taller than I am and I got more than a glimpse. It was Lance Hurley!"

Lance. She had never vaguely considered Lance. But of course! How stupid could she be? In her preoccupation with Mr. Drake as the prime suspect, she had lost sight entirely of Lance's position in the case, and one of the things that had helped throw her off cue—Mr. Calder's avowal of Lance's fondness for Mary-anne—was suddenly the most damaging. Carrie Calder must have been cognizant of that fondness, and, in spite of the old lady's opinion of his father, Lance was a natural choice for her to have entrusted with the Queens. Lance had shown an abnormal interest at her gasp when she'd been up the chimney and he'd made a point of staying behind when she left the supply room. Later, she noticed soot on his sleeve. . . . It made sense, unpleasant sense. And now—

"Connie," Happy said, drawing her to a halt under the street lamp. Do you realize that for the past hour we've been playing Sherlock Holmes and his friend Watson? And although you may know why, I don't! You said you'd explain."

"Oh, Happy, I'm sorry. I never did tell you what else was on the smoke shelf along with the kittens, did I?" As she had done for Aunt Bet, she related the finding of the circles and their subsequent obliteration. "You see, Hap, someone erased the clue that proved they had been hidden and not simply given away."

Happy nodded thoughtfully, then said slowly, "Connie, you surprise me. I figured this figurine deal was a lot of nonsense, but now— Well, it does seem as though they've been swiped!"

"Exactly. And it must have been by someone who knew about finding the kittens. That's the list I mentioned while we were dancing—the list of suspects."

"And I'm on it!" Happy grinned, but the momentary twinkle in his brown eyes died almost immediately. Connie knew that he no longer considered the mystery of the Queens a laughing matter.

"Oh, dear," she sighed regretfully, "Lance was so nice with the kittens. I just can't think of him as a thief."

"Maybe he's a schizo—split personality—a Jekyll and Hyde," Happy suggested.

Happy could be right. Lance did have a peculiar background.

"Oh, Hap, here's the alley. Let's go back to the house and see what's up." She said it gaily, hoping Happy would consider it a game. Mike, by turning out the light and locking the shed, had deprived her of any other valid reason.

"No, ma'm! As an escort, how can I face your aunt as it is? And when I realize what might have happened, especially in that dark house, I get all shook up."

"We've got to go back!" Connie argued earnestly, a new and startling idea striking her. "Lance lives with his mother in a small apartment. Maybe he couldn't take the Queens there. Maybe he stole them from the fireplace and hid them somewhere else"—she recalled Mike's statement about tools aplenty—"maybe he had been hunting a tool in the supply room so that he could get at them. Happy, they may still be around the place! Lance may come back again—"

She broke off, noting Happy's totally unimpressed mein. His eyes narrowed into a male "I'm-taking-over-from-here" expression and the pressure on her arm tightened as he guided her toward the car.

Connie gave up. She did not want to make a scene. The eight-o'clock lull had ended, people were appearing now on the street, returning from dinner and early movies. Apparently the office party had broken up. Several of the parked cars were starting to roll. Furthermore, Happy had a point.

"Oh, Hap," she teased, "you remind me of the dog we owned before Ruggles. He was so protective he wouldn't even let us go swimming. When we wanted to have fun, we left him home."

"So?" Happy made growling animal noises and Connie laughed.

"I didn't mean it that way," she protested. It was impossible to get really angry with Happy, although she was seriously concerned about leaving the Fifth Street house unattended.

"It's eight-fifty," Happy announced, glancing at his watch. "In ten minutes the watchman will be on duty."

"Watchman?"

"Sure, you see, this section of town has been partly reclaimed, but not many blocks away it's not—well, top drawer. And, as Mike said, there's a lot of valuable equipment stowed at Calder's just for the taking. Also, there are vandals who'd break in just for kicks."

"Well," Connie mused, "I learn something every minute." She had never thought of a watchman before, and naturally had never seen him.

But it occurred to her that if Drake had not let her out of the cellar the night Butterfield had locked her in by mistake the watchman would have released her.

"The watchman is a retired prison guard," Happy continued, "and he's dead serious about this present job. Keeps a night book on the mantel in the living room and everyone who comes in when he's on duty has to sign it—even Mr. Calder."

Connie was relieved. A prison guard sounded adequate to any situation and it was unlikely that Lance, in the short time elapsing between her toss over the wall, Mike's locking up, and the watchman's arrival, would risk returning for the Queens.

"I wonder," Happy pondered as he opened the car door, "how Lance will react toward us on Monday? Do you suppose Emily Post has the proper greeting for a girl whose neck you almost broke and for a man you led a merry chase?"

"I don't know," Connie replied absently. The word Monday had started her thinking. Between now and Monday there was Sunday, a whole day when the house would be empty—a whole day that Lance could have to himself, uninterrupted.

Tomorrow she'd come back to Fifth Street. But she did not mention her plan to Happy.

THE bus ride downtown was agonizingly slow. Either the driver was ahead of schedule or drugged by the Sunday lassitude that hung over the city, for he made no attempt to catch the green lights, which he could have done easily with a slight acceleration of speed.

Connie glanced at her watch. It was one o'clock, a full half hour since she had left Aunt Bet outside the church and started for Fifth Street. Normally the entire ride took less than twenty minutes. She squirmed impatiently as they waited for the *Go* signal at Tenth and Chestnut.

Back at the apartment last night when she and Happy had raided the refrigerator and discussed the mystery, Happy had reasserted that the man he had chased was Lance. But now Connie wasn't

131

sure he was right. She kept remembering the figure she had seen dart from the alley. The man had been shorter than Lance, more Drake's build.

Connie sighed. Instinctively, she was turning her suspicions back to Drake, doing mental handsprings to avoid thinking ill of Lance. The man she had seen may well have been a total stranger, with nothing whatsoever to do with the mystery. If only, if only, she had gotten a glimpse of the man who had thrown her over the wall. It must have been the same one Happy had been chasing, because he was breathing heavily, as though he had been running hard.

But whether Happy was right or wrong, and whether the person who had stolen the Queens was Lance, or Drake, or someone she had not yet thought of, Connie was convinced of one thing —the Queens were still somewhere around the old house. All the events to date pointed to that assumption. Whoever had been Miss Calder's trusted agent in hiding the figurines had quite possibly decided they were as safe there as anywhere. Since there had been no police investigation of the property, he could simply bide his time and negotiate for their disposal or wait until the excitement about them died down to take them away.

And last night Happy had mentioned a very pertinent point. Before Drake's search there had been a question of demolishing the old outbuilding instead of using it for a supply room. The demolition talk, then, had been responsible for the Queens' removal from their original place on the smoke shelf, which, as hiding places went, was ingenious.

The new place also must be ingenious, Connie reflected, to have skipped Drake's notice unless, of course, he had put them there himself.

Whatever the chain of circumstances, the culprit's plans had misfired and waiting no longer suited him. He wanted to get at the figurines. In fact he was desperate, for only a desperate person would have pushed her over the churchyard wall and run the risk of being tracked down on a charge more serious than larceny.

Connie smiled to herself. In the cemetery Happy had joked about a ghost causing a concussion. He had referred to the man under the tombstone on which she had hit her head, but Happy had thought of the wrong ghost. The ghost who was indirectly responsible for the present lump underneath her brown felt hat was old Carrie Calder.

Connie got off the bus and hurried down Fifth Street, skirting the group of tourists who were assembling on the sidewalk for a tour of Independence Hall. Without a key, she had no idea how she would get into the house, but the important thing was to get there, be on the spot. She worried that even now she might be too late. The criminal had had all morning to accomplish his purpose.

Nearing the house, she decided that the simplest approach to getting in was the obvious—

try the front door. She walked up the steps and turned the knob. The door opened at her touch.

Although the unlocked door spelled anything but nefarious doings inside, she entered the hall apprehensively. The sound of pounding in the basement made her heart skip momentarily. Then she recognized men's voices, loud and hearty, with no attempt at secrecy.

"Who's there?" she called down the cellar stairs.

The pounding stopped. *"We're* here," someone replied, laughing. "Who are you?"

"Connie Blair, the girl who's doing the art work."

Footsteps started across the cellar and the familiar whisker-stubbled face of the plumber on the job appeared at the bottom of the stairs. "Hi, Connie. We're hooking up the new heater. Had to do it on the week end because the heat had to be off. Why are you here?"

"I came to feed the cat." It was partly true.

"Oh, well, we'll be through in about ten minutes. Been here since the crack of dawn. Want us to wait and lock up after puss has her chow?"

"No," Connie replied hastily, not wanting to lose the opportunity of being here alone. "No, I'll lock up."

If the workmen had been here since that early hour, the thief could have had no chance to unearth the prize. Still, he might turn up later and she had plenty to do in the interim. Feeding the cat could wait another ten minutes or so.

First she glanced at the night book, which, as

Happy had predicted, was on the mantel above the living-room fireplace. The page marked with Saturday's date was blank. No one, then, had entered the house after the watchman had come on duty. She closed the book and shivered. Despite the temperature, which was far warmer than the day of Happy's fire, the house was chilly. But the new oil burner would soon warm it up.

Happy's fire! Drake's fury! Had Drake moved the Queens from one smoke ledge to another? Was that why he'd been so incensed when he'd seen the burning wood?

Quickly she bent down and looked up the flue, but saw immediately that a damper, probably a more recent addition, closed off the opening. The damper opened only a few inches, not nearly wide enough for the figurines to have been pushed through.

Disappointed, Connie started on a systematic search of the house. But nowhere could she discover a possible hiding place that would have escaped the omnipresent hammers and saws of the remodeling. The still-beautiful, random-width floors, the carved mantels, the majestic staircase had not been touched in the renovation, but they gave no sign whatsoever of having been tampered with, or of concealing secret panels.

In the downstairs hall she noticed that the sponge pinned across the cherry print had dried out. Momentarily, interest in her paid job took precedence over her voluntary detective work. Carefully she pulled out the bottom pins, lifted the sponge, and looked underneath. A thin strip of the cherry print had peeled off disclosing a faded, but exotic, paper of Chinese birds and flowers. What fun it would be to reproduce to-morrow—provided, tomorrow, she was all in one piece. Gingerly she raised her hand and felt the bump on her head.

"We're going now, Connie," the plumber told her, coming up from the cellar, followed by two men in coveralls. "By the way," he said, scratching his beard, "how can you feed the cat? The key to the supply room's missing."

Connie glanced at the hook beside the rear door. Whoever had taken the key last night had not returned it.

"Well," the plumber said, "you figure that one. It's lucky for Calder Company, though, that heater men always bring their own tools."

Connie went out into the garden. The key had a large identifying label attached to it with heavy brown string and shouldn't be hard to find if it had been dropped somewhere in haste. But although she examined every foot of the ground, felt beneath borders of ivy, searched under all the bushes, it did not turn up. Neither was it anywhere on the porch.

In closing the door to the supply room last night, the spring lock probably caught and Mike might have locked the key inside. With her nose pressed against the pane, Connie peered through the window. The infiltrating light made the room reasonably bright. But she could not see the key lying anywhere. Probably it still was in the culprit's possession.

One other thing claimed her attention, however—the heavy tools, the picks, axes, shovels, which Mr. Butterfield always kept neatly stacked near the fireplace, were in confusion, as though someone had tried hurriedly to select a particular one.

The jumble of tools established in her mind the role of the supply room in the mystery of last night. The thief had been hunting something with which to extricate the figurines—a tool heavy enough to break through solid construction. And the installation of the heater might well account for his haste in trying to get at them, provided he had secreted them in the basement near the old furnace.

Certainly, if that were the case, he must have been frantic about the cache and would come to see what had happened after the workmen were out of the way. In fact, he might arrive at any minute . . .

Going back to the house, Connie quickly locked both doors. The thief had already demonstrated his ability to enter the property and it was essential that the place looked closed up and empty. With the workmen gone, and no evidence that they had happened upon the Queens, the thief undoubtedly would not let the golden opportunity of an afternoon, supposedly alone, slip by without taking them from their hiding place. He had proved his urgency last night, and his apprehensiveness on Friday by obliterating the circles in the soot.

Hastily, Connie started upstairs, devising a plan. She would hide on the second floor until he had gotten the necessary tools from the supply room and gone into the basement. Then she would tiptoe down to the top of the cellar stairs and listen for—and watch, if she could see without being seen—his removal of the Queens. When she was positive he was almost finished, she'd throw the bolt on the door and—presto!—he'd be imprisoned with the loot.

On the landing Connie stopped. She didn't really believe the Queens were in the basement. Secreting them behind stone or brick would have been too major an operation not to have left a telltale scar. Connie was no novice at sighting such clues, and she had seen nothing unusual when she had examined the floor, the walls, and even the ceiling. No, the solid basement had not felt the scrape of a chisel, the blow of a pick for years.

Recalling the stack of newspapers in the cellar, Connie retraced her steps. If the stored data were of interest to Carrie Calder, it could be important in the pattern of the mystery. Whether the thief did or did not come to the house today, this was *her* golden opportunity to look around.

The workmen who had installed the oil burner also had put a new bulb in the dangling socket. Carefully, since it was impossible to bolt the door from the inner side, she inserted a small wedge of wood she had picked up from shavings in the hall to keep it closed. At night the crack of light would have shown under the sill, but in the daytime it was hardly noticeable.

The new oil burner exuded a comforting warmth, and, unlike the one she was accustomed to in Meadowbrook which thumped and grumbled in its complaining old age, it was running with a minimum of noise. Over its soft, homey murmur she'd be able to hear anyone walking in the hall above. The basement was as good a place as any to keep her vigil.

Since the night she had been locked in here, there had been a change. The debris which had littered the floor had been swept into a corner, so that the heater men would not have to track across it. The newspapers were still stacked along the wall, but the piles labeled WORLD WAR II and DEATH NOTICES OF INTEREST had a ruffled-through aspect. Connie could account for the condition of WORLD WAR II for she had done it herself, but she could not remember touching DEATH NOTICES OF INTEREST. Squatting on her heels, she examined the pile more closely.

Unlike the others, which were complete issues of the newspapers, DEATH NOTICES OF INTEREST contained only single sheets, cut with precision along the fold of the spread. On each sheet someone—undoubtedly Miss Calder—had circled the obituary of interest with bright-red crayon and had drawn an arrow ending at the lower half of the page where, with the same crayon, she had written her personal opinion of the deceased.

Connie was amused. The first notice concerned a woman who had died accidentally. Miss Calder's comment was cryptic: *Never did know her limitations. Skiing at sixty!* The next was about a man who had collapsed in his office: *Good bridge player,* Miss Calder had written. Of a young girl, she said simply: *Sweet child,* and about a captain in the Navy, *Intelligent and brave.*

If the sheets once had been piled chronologically, they were now in complete disorder, as though someone had tossed them onto the floor, then shuffled them back like a deck of playing cards. Connie leafed through them, hoping to find a name or incident with a meaning. About midway from the top of the stack, she came across a sheet, torn in half. Except for the last line, the obituary to which the arrow pointed was missing, but Miss Calder's notation at the bottom of the page was intact:

My one mistake in life. I should have married him when he asked me.

Connie glanced at the last line, underscored by the lower arc of the red circle that had surrounded the full item—apparently, instead of succumbing to heartbreak over Carrie's refusal, he had married someone else, for it read: *Survived by his son, Andrew.*

Who was Andrew? Had Drake's father been Carrie Calder's regretted beau?

Above her, in the hall, Connie heard footsteps. Jamming the torn paper into the pocket of the coat she had not bothered to take off, she listened breathlessly, expecting the sound to continue past the entrance to the basement and on out to the back porch. Instead, at the cellar door, they halted.

Connie was trapped. There was no time to figure out who the person on the other side of the door could be. If it was the thief, and the Queens were hidden in the basement after all, it was paramount that she hide and watch operations. The lighted bulb might not forewarn the culprit of her presence. It was quite likely that he would suppose the men who had installed the furnace had forgotten to turn it off. Nevertheless, he'd be sure to give at least a cursory glance around to make sure he was alone.

She ran toward the cold room, the arch now completely visible under the new bulb. But, to her chagrin, the little room was fairly well illuminated and the stark brick walls gave her no chance of concealment.

She had to find something to hide *behind*. To the right of the arch there was a space about two feet wide between the wall and the back of the oil burner. Before she squeezed into it, she listened again.

There was no sound from the hall. In the silence Connie had a sudden, paralyzing thought. Had the person suspected that she was in the basement? Had he slipped the bolt, imprisoning her and allowing himself freedom to remove the Queens from some other part of the house and to disappear with them into thin air forever?

Almost with relief, Connie heard the creak of the door as it was opened. She saw trousered legs start down the stairs. Wriggling behind the oil burner, she crouched over so that she was completely obscured from view and waited.

The person, still unknown to her because she could not risk exposure by so much as a peek in his direction, circled the rear of the cellar, then approached the heater—headed, she surmised, for the cold room.

Connie wished fervently that she had backed into her confined space so that she faced the arch. In her crouched position, with her head bent to her chest, her own body obstructed the view of the arch. Holding her breath, she prayed that the intruder would not look to his right, whoever he was—but the steps came closer, then abruptly stopped.

"Better come out from there, Connie, or you'll roast."

It was Lance Hurley's voice.

CHAPTER 13

On Account of a Rabbit

CONNIE backed out from behind the oil burner and confronted Lance. He was standing, hands on his hips, looking at her with a kind of resigned exasperation, like a father who has just caught a child in an act of wrongdoing he had fully expected the youngster to commit.

His vexed manner interested her. It was an odd attitude to assume toward her if he was the one who had almost broken her neck the night before.

"I don't even need to ask what you're doing here," Lance sighed. "Yesterday, when I delivered some prints to your art director at Reid and Renshaw, we had quite a talk about you. You consider yourself quite an amateur detective, don't you?"

There seemed no adequate answer and Connie made none. In the short silence that ensued, the

143

click of a turning key in the front door was clearly audible, and simultaneously Lance's manner changed. He ran for the steps, his long legs taking them two at a time, and hissed over his shoulder a curt order to Connie.

"Don't move and don't make a sound!"

Before she had a chance to do either, she heard Lance speak again from the top of the stairs. "Hi, Andy," he said pleasantly. "What brings you here on a Sunday?"

Connie thought of the line from Shakespeare— "One man in his time plays many parts." In less than two minutes Lance had changed his outward mien three times.

"Why, hello, Lance. I stopped by to see about the new oil burner. If it's not working right, you know, I'll want it attended to before we pay the bill. I'm staying only a few minutes. And I presume you came here on a Sunday to feed the—the little newcomers?"

"Yes, Andy, I came to feed them—the mother, of course. And so did Miss Blair. But when I told her about the new oil burner—well, we decided to have a look-see. Come on up, Connie," Lance called, his voice smooth as silk.

Lance was lying and Connie wondered what his game was, and what Drake's reaction would be at again discovering her in the basement. Would he explode or take this opportunity to be obsequiously polite, make up for his rudeness the day of Happy's fire, when Lance had defended her?

"Why, Miss Blair," Drake said as she came into the room, "that's admirable—I mean, to be so interested in the affairs of the Calder firm, especially when you don't actually work for us."

Connie was amazed. Was the man really serious? Did his loyalty extend—

The telephone interrupted further talk for the moment. Lance picked it up from beneath the coat bench.

"No. . . . Yes. . . . Yes. Yes, I'll tell her." He replaced the instrument. "Connie, that was your aunt—"

"Aunt Bet?" Connie asked anxiously when Lance hesitated as though he had information he didn't want to impart.

"Yes, your aunt Bet. She's ill and wants you home. If I had a car—"

"I have a car parked outside," Drake volunteered. "I'll be glad to drive you, Miss Blair. After all, it won't take long."

Feeling about Drake as she did, Connie was reluctant to accept a favor from him, but she was concerned about her aunt. Elizabeth Easton was no sissy. If she had called Connie home, it must be serious, and taxis, on Sundays, were hard to come by. "Why, thank you, Mr. Drake. That's very kind."

"Oh, by the way, Connie," Lance said as she started for the door, "your art director sent you a message. The Sansom people have enough data now for their new line, so after you finish the last paper, you're to report back to the office."

No sooner were they headed west than Connie realized that Drake's generous offer of the ride had been prompted by an ulterior motive, and it was connected with the Queens.

"Miss Blair," he said casually, "I haven't seen you since the little . . . ah . . . family was found in the chimney. Butterfield tells me you found them on the smoke shelf. Is that correct?"

"Yes."

"Well . . . er . . . you didn't find anything else up there, did you, Miss Blair?"

"Like what, Mr. Drake?"

Drake coughed a laugh, as though the whole conversation was really quite trivial. "Like the little matter we discussed once before—the matter of Maryanne's inheritance."

"If you mean did I find the figurines—no, Mr. Drake, I didn't."

"Oh. Well, I was a bit concerned. You see, Miss Blair"—again he coughed his synthetic laugh—"I will admit something to you. I did miss the smoke shelf in my search. In fact, I'll admit something else—I didn't know chimneys *had* smoke ledges."

"And that," Connie told herself as she left him at the curb, "is exactly what I would maintain if I'd stolen a priceless treasure."

Aunt Bet was not in the apartment. Connie expected to find her in bed, but there was no evidence that she had even lain down, for the heavy candlewick spread was as neat and tidy as when they had left for church. Neither was there any indication that Aunt Bet had made herself a cup of tea—her panacea for all ailments.

Then what had happened? Had she met with an accident on the street? Had the call come from a hospital, and if so, which one? Had Lance misconstrued the message?

Connie was agitated, but she checked her first impulse to call the police for a check on accident cases. Instead, she dialed Earle Filmore. Perhaps he knew something.

"Where's Elizabeth?" came the response. "Why, she's at the art museum, Constance. I talked with her not five minutes ago. I asked her to ring me if the exhibit of Chinese gardens was worth seeing. On her unqualified approbation, I'm on my way there now."

Connie sat back, weak from the mental strain and furious. Lance had tricked her. He had wanted her out of the house on Fifth Street and he'd used the first available hoax that presented itself. But who had telephoned—

The telephone in the apartment rang and jolted her out of her speculative thoughts. It was Mr. Renshaw.

"Connie," he asked without preamble, "have you a key to the Calder mansion? The Sansom people are in town for a business convention and they'd like to see the place. They're from the Midwest, you know, and they've read about the Mall and old Philadelphia houses. This is the only day they have to spare and I hate to bother Calder on Sunday, but . . ."

But the client must be served, Connie smiled to herself, or he'll take his account elsewhere. "I haven't a key, Mr. Renshaw, but I think I can dig one up. Shall I call you back?"

"Only if you can't. I'm in the client's suite at the Bellevue. If I don't hear from you in ten minutes, we'll start on down."

"All right, Mr. Renshaw."

"And, Connie, it's not necessary for you to be there. Just get us in."

The simplest procedure was first to call the house. Drake might have gone back. Of course, if Lance were there alone, he might not, for obvious reasons, even answer. As a final resort, she could try Happy at his fraternity house.

But the last was unnecessary, for Happy was the one who answered her call to Fifth Street. "Hey," he demanded, recognizing her voice at once, "where the dickens are *you?*"

"Home."

"Well, you weren't there an hour ago. I called."

"No, I was at Fifth Street."

"But I called here, too. I got Lance. He said he hadn't seen you."

"Happy, he was lying—"

"I was afraid of that. Our conversation didn't make sense—too scrambled to suit me. I was sure you'd come here today the minute you got a chance. That's why I hotfooted down to protect you, ungrateful wretch that you are, from being maybe burned up in the coal furnace. After the toss over the wall, I don't exactly trust our Mr. Hurley."

"I couldn't have been burned in the coal furnace because it's no longer there. Anyway, thanks for the kind thought. I'll explain the details later, but first, Hap, listen . . ."

Quickly she told him of Mr. Renshaw's request. "Hap, will you let them in and—and—would you do me a big favor?"

"Try me and see!"

"Will you stick with the Sansom people while they're there? Sort of play host? They don't know much about the Restoration and Mr. Renshaw would appreciate it if someone could explain—"

"And Mr. Renshaw would appreciate Miss Blair, of the agency, supplying the guide, eh? Okay, Connie, I'll put it right with the boss. I'll do something else for you, too."

"What's that?"

"I'll stay around the house after they've gone— until the watchman comes on duty. It will save you the trouble of making a second trip downtown. After all, I can hide as well as you can, and although I haven't had your experience"—Happy's voice was deadly serious, but Connie could tell he was grinning—"I think I can apprehend your criminal, especially with the help of a length of lead pipe I see before me."

"Oh, stop it!" Connie had intended to go back to Fifth Street, but it was now close to five o'clock. If the Sansom people stayed an hour or more—well, the thief wasn't likely to make an attempt for the Queens tonight. From all indications, it was a job that required time. And, if anything came up, Happy was on deck. "Was Lance there when you arrived, Hap?"

"Yes, he sort of appeared out of the woodwork. Now he's gone out to the garden and I'm alone in the house like a stuffed owl in a forgotten attic."

Connie stretched out on the sofa to think. The constant seesaw of the scales, first pointing to Drake as the prime suspect, then to Lance, was wearing her down, and getting her no nearer her real objective of finding the Queens. If she failed in that, not only Maryanne Jessup—although she had warned Connie to keep clear of the mystery—but the Calder twins, too, would be frightfully disappointed.

The Calder twins, she mused, were a cute pair. She hoped they'd gotten a new pet to replace the dead rabbit.

The dead rabbit!

Connie swung her feet to the floor and sat up stiffly. The dead rabbit that Jeff, the chauffeur, was unable to bury because of the frozen ground! Of course, of course—

"Anybody home?" Aunt Bet called from the foyer.

"Yes, I am. And, oh, Aunt Bet—" Connie jumped up to meet her aunt, anxious to tell her the startling conjecture she had just made.

But Elizabeth Easton was not alone. She had Earle Filmore in tow along with two women who had gone to the museum with her. They were full of the exhibition and starving hungry.

"Help me get a snack together, will you, Connie?" Aunt Bet asked.

"We'll all help," one of the women offered, and after they had removed their coats, they jammed into the tiny kitchenette.

Too many cooks made it an almost endless job to assemble the "snack" and no one but Connie was in a hurry. She couldn't be rude and rush her aunt's guests, but once the food was on the table she gulped a cold-cut sandwich, a pickle, a piece of cake, and before the others had finished, excused herself and raced out to the corner drugstore to telephone. It was impossible to talk in the apartment against the babble about the beauty of the Chinese gardens, and she had to get in touch with Happy.

Crossing the street she was stopped by a loud wolf whistle. Turning, she saw the green convertible rounding the corner. Happy pulled up to the curb.

"Going somewhere, miss?"

"Oh, Hap," Connie remonstrated, getting into the car. "You said you'd stay at the house until the watchman came on duty, and—"

"He came early," Happy told her, backing the car to the front of the apartment. "It seems," he continued, switching off the ignition, "he had a little trouble last night, so—"

"What kind of trouble?" Connie demanded eagerly.

"Oh, about midnight he chased somebody out of the garden."

"Happy, that proves it! The Queens are buried in the garden!"

"Hold it! You lost me somewhere back there. What makes you so sure they are buried?"

"Because of the dead rabbit."

"The *what?*"

"The Calder twins' pet. It died and couldn't be buried easily on account of the frozen ground. In reverse, the Queens couldn't be dug up without a lot of trouble. But now that we've hit a warm spell—well, the thief wants to get at them before we have another freeze. And it's just simple arithmetic that the Queens must be in the garden, since they certainly aren't anywhere in the house."

"I'll concede they might be around the property," Happy admitted. "All that fracas last night —well, it proves somebody was looking for something. And probably you're right, that they *are* in the garden. But who buried them?"

"I don't know," Connie said frankly. "Are you sure it was Lance you were chasing last night?"

"Yes, positive!" Happy was emphatic.

"But, Hap," Connie insisted, "I saw a shorter man running, more Mr. Drake's build. I can't be sure Lance isn't the culprit. He's certainly been acting odd lately, and for some reason he used a very cruel hoax to get me away from Fifth Street this afternoon—he said Aunt Bet was ill and needed me.

"But, on the other hand, Mr. Drake has been insistent from the beginning that the Queens were given away, and he made a distinct point of questioning me about the smoke shelf when he drove me back to the apartment. Besides, he would have been a natural choice for carrying out Miss Calder's plan of hiding the figurines—and he knew about the question of demolishing the outbuilding, while Lance may not. Still, I can't figure his motive. He appears to be a man who puts self-esteem above money, and certainly he's no art collector. Happy, did anything happen at the house while you were there?"

Happy didn't answer directly. Instead, with a studied casualness that Connie had learned to connect with Happy when he had something really important up his sleeve, he said, "It's a shame old Carrie gave away that celebrated coffee service."

"The what?"

"Yep, a real shame she gave it away. Besides playing host to the tribe from the corn belt, I had a lot of other visitors. I could have used that set to serve refreshments."

A breeze with more bite in it than she had felt for the last two days blew Connie's hair across her eyes. She brushed it back with her hand and stared at him. "Happy Wallace, what are you driving at?"

"Give me a chance . . . please, princess. While the Sansom people were touring the house, Butterfield came in to stoke the furnace—he said he

didn't know the new oil burner was installed.
Then Lance wandered in the back door, and
Drake came in the front way. After the whole en-
tourage left, I was about to lock up when some
character walked into the hall, said he was looking
for Andy, said he had business with him. Connie,"
—for one of the few times since she had known
Happy, she heard the bantering tone leave his
voice—"if the business that bird had with Andy
Drake is connected with the figurines, we're not
batting in the Little League."

"Meaning?"

"That I didn't like his looks." Happy was completely serious. "He had a nasty eye—sinister
might be the word—like a bad horse, and he was
straight out of a gangster novel. I've grown accustomed to your face, Connie. I'd hate to see it
scarred with acid. Promise Uncle Happy you'll
quit the rackets? Don't tangle with Public Enemy
Number One . . . pul-eeze!"

Connie didn't reply immediately. The figurines
hadn't been dug up yet, for she had been over the
whole garden this afternoon looking for the key
to the supply room. There was no sign of the
ground having been turned over. It was undis-
turbed, just as the frost had sealed it before the
thaw. There was still too good a chance to save
the Queens to give up now.

"No, I can't promise, Hap," she said thoughtfully. "I'm sorry, but I just can't."

"Okay, then. Get back to the apartment. I've
studying to do. And don't worry about the Queens

disappearing tonight. Our watchman doesn't scare easy."

Connie got out of the car, sensing the sudden abruptness of his manner. "I wish," she demurred, "the cat had been fed."

"She was," Happy said coldly. "I did it."

"But the key, Hap— Where did you find the key to the supply room?"

Happy started the engine. "On the board by the rear door."

"Then one of your visitors this afternoon must have replaced it," Connie called after him as he drove off, "because it wasn't there earlier." But Happy gave no indication that he had heard.

Connie climbed the stairs slowly. For the first time, Happy had asked a favor—one for her own good—and she had refused him so bluntly. Now he was angry. He had left without even a backward glance, and the thought that he might never ask her for another date depressed her.

Aunt Bet and her friends were listening to the hi-fi. Connie took the torn-out obituary notice from her coat pocket, bade them good night, and went into her room.

Before she undressed, she spread the paper on her bureau and stared at it. The date was missing, but judging from the clothes on the characters in a cartoon strip on the reverse side, it looked to be about ten years old.

What, if anything, she wondered, did the notice have to do with the mystery?

CHAPTER 14

Sinister Apology

*The world would sleep if things were run
By men who said "It can't be done!"*

AFTER lunch on Monday Connie resumed her place before the Chinese bird-and-flower print, repeating over and over to herself the adage her father always recited when any particularly vexing problem faced the family. But the lines seemed to have lost their power to charm. They gave her no renewed productive thinking, no new slant on the mystery of the Queens.

The print, which at first glance had looked so intricate, was actually quite simple to reproduce. Even if she dawdled, she'd finish it this afternoon. Tomorrow she'd be back behind her desk at Reid and Renshaw with no excuse thereafter to go down to Fifth Street. Time, in her quest for the missing figurines, was running out.

The frustrating part was that Connie was sure they were in the garden and the thief was working in the house. All she lacked was the one vital clue that would tie them together. For, unless the thief led Connie to them, she didn't know where to dig, and she couldn't uproot the entire place on the basis of a supposition. She needed a big break, something which would force his hand.

At noon, Connie had called Maryanne from a pay station about the obituary notice. Despite Maryanne's firm command that Connie stay out of the mystery, she was definitely interested in the find. She had discussed the whole situation with Mr. Calder over the week end, she said, and gotten nowhere. She could throw no light on Miss Calder's old beau, nor on whom the surviving Andrew might be, and laughed off the possibility of Mr. Drake. But she promised to interrogate the family, including Nellie, and see if they could come up with anything constructive. If not, she told Connie, she would track down the notice in the newspaper morgue. Unfortunately, she had a date with the twins to go Christmas shopping that afternoon, so the morgue research would have to wait until tomorrow.

It was the best Connie could hope for, since she herself could not leave her job on such an errand.

"Connie, for you." Lance's voice from the stairs startled her. He was holding the telephone toward her at the end of the long cord and Connie realized she had been so immersed in her thoughts that she hadn't heard it ring. "Don't get up. I'll bring it down."

He handed her the telephone and went on into the living room where she could see him setting up his equipment near the window.

"Hello," she said, half expecting it to be Mr. Renshaw asking how she was coming along with her work.

"Miss Blair, this is Nellie. Do you remember me?"

"Oh, Nellie." It took Connie a second to adjust to the surprise. "Why, of course. I met you last Friday on our way to the Calders."

"That's right, and in the car you mentioned you liked to garden. Miss Blair, now that the weather has moderated for a spell, would you mind doing me a great favor? Would you mind digging up a little bush for me?"

"No, Nellie, I'd be happy to," Connie assured her. "Which one is it?"

"The Vitex micro—" Connie couldn't catch the last word. "Mr. Calder says I may have it for my place out here in Flourtown. You won't really have to dig at all, Miss Blair. The shrub is shallow-rooted, anyway, and only a baby. Just slip a trowel under it gently and it will lift out. And thank you so much."

Her voice trailed off and Connie was afraid she'd hang up satisfied that she had completed her instructions and adequately voiced her appreciation.

"Wait, Nellie! I'm not sure which bush the Vitex is. They're all just bare branches now. Tell me its exact location."

"Oh . . . of course . . . it's near the umbrella tree in the corner of the end wall . . . about three feet to the left toward the street. I think it has a wooden tag on it you still might be able to read."

"Oh, yes." Connie could picture the little shrub quite well now. "But won't I disturb the new bulbs?"

"New bulbs? What new bulbs?" Clearly, Nellie was puzzled.

"The new tulip bulbs you had planted this fall. Mike said he saw a man putting them in, just about where the bush is."

Nellie protested. "Oh, no, Mike must be mistaken. Those new bulbs are along the edge of the porch and I put them in myself. I can't imagine what Mike's talking about—anyhow, I must ring off because this is costing money. Just wet the roots and wrap them in newspaper and leave the bush in the hall, Miss Blair. Mr. Calder will stop by for it this evening. He's picking up the twins in town—they've gone Christmas shopping . . ."

Despite Nellie's assertion that the toll call was costing money, she rambled on, but Connie paid slight heed to her account of the twins' shopping spree. She was watching Lance. Since the mention of the bulbs, he hadn't moved a muscle. His rigid back was evidence that he was listening to Connie's end of the conversation.

When Nellie hung up, Connie said precisely into the dead instrument so that Lance wouldn't miss a word:

"I'm glad there are no bulbs in the bed, Nellie, for that gives me a chance to dig *deep and wide* and protect the roots of the Vitex."

Then she replaced the 'phone in its cradle and smiled with satisfaction. Poor Nellie, she'd have argued the point if she'd heard. It was a great deal more than "just slip a trowel under it."

Connie pushed the telephone under the bench. The break had come, the clue she'd been waiting for. Now she knew *where* to dig in the garden. Beyond a doubt, the man whom Mike had thought he'd seen planting the bulbs had been burying the figurines. If the stage setting she was planning didn't produce the figurines, and, at the same time, smoke out the thief, Mike could be contacted later for a description.

The time to dig would be after five o'clock. Before then, with everyone around, her quarry might decide to forgo his loot and remain anonymous. But if she were alone in the garden . . .

"I'm going to dig up a bush for Nellie after working hours," she called brightly to Lance. "Won't it be fun gardening in December?"

Lance didn't turn around, and several seconds elapsed before he answered with a noncommittal shrug, "If you like gardening, I suppose it will."

Connie put her sketch block on the chair, with the brush and water pan beside it, and went in search of Mr. Drake. Her project needed advertising. No possible suspect must be left in ignorance of what she intended to do. She found Drake on the second floor talking with Butterfield.

"Mr. Drake," she asked, flashing him her sweetest smile, "I'd like to ask your permission about something when you're free."

Drake's self-importance responded immediately to the flattery. "I can spare you a moment right now, Miss Blair. What is it you want?"

Connie told him of Nellie's request, adding, "I thought I'd wait until I've finished my work . . . until after five. It gets dark so early this time of year, so may I use the kerosene lantern in the supply room to see by?"

Drake did not reply directly. "Where is the bush?" he countered.

"In the bed at the end of the wall." Connie pointed out the window, watching Drake carefully. But it was impossible to tell from his reactions whether there was any ulterior motive beyond his question or whether it was simply part of his "I-must-know-every-detail" character. She explained: "It's small, but I want to take a good ball of earth with it to protect its roots."

"The ground's awfully heavy after this frost, Miss Blair. Why not let me have one of the men do it? I'll supervise it, personally, if you'd like," he offered with unaccustomed graciousness.

"Oh, no," Connie protested. "Nellie asked me especially. And I love to garden."

"Well, if you insist. And you have my permission to use the lantern."

"Thank you, Mr. Drake," she responded, turning to go, when Butterfield touched her on the arm.

"I didn't mean to butt in," he said, walking with her toward the stairs, "but I couldn't help overhearing. I'll dig it up, Miss Blair. There's no point in your getting all dirty again."

Mr. Butterfield's gallantry in insisting on climbing the chimney had almost been responsible for her not finding the circles in the soot. At this crucial stage, she had no intention of letting it prevent her finding the Queens.

"No, don't bother. Just leave the supply room and the rear door open for me. I'll lock up."

On her way downstairs she saw Mr. Calder about to leave by the front door.

"Mr. Calder!" she called from the landing. "What time will you be back for the Vitex?"

If things got rough in the garden, she could always scream for help, and if Mr. Calder was there, to see for himself what was going on, so much the better.

He looked up at her, frowning. "About six, Miss Blair. But it was presumptuous of Nellie to ask you to dig up the bush. You forget it. I'll do it when I get here."

"Oh, no, Mr. Calder. I will. I'd love to. But if I haven't finished by the time you come back, please look for me in the garden."

Mr. Calder nodded. "But don't stay out there longer than necessary, Miss Blair. Our watchman has had trouble with prowlers."

Connie sat down in front of the print. By ten minutes to five it was completed. She gathered her materials to take home and laid them on the window sill, sorry that the job at the house was over. She had been sorry, too, she realized, all day, that Happy hadn't put in his usual appearance. If he had, she might have been able to patch up their difference of the night before.

As the workmen began to leave, Connie found herself holding an impromptu reception in the hall. Having heard she was leaving, each one stopped and wished her luck. After they had gone, Connie got her coat and started for the supply room.

Shortly after her conversation with Nellie, Lance had vanished. So far as she knew, only Drake was still in the building, somewhere on the second floor. Butterfield was not in the supply room, but its untidy condition, the tools in disarray, were evidence that he was still around.

"I hope he goes soon," she said to herself.

Like an automaton, Connie fed the mother cat from the remaining can that Happy had dropped on the porch. Then she lighted the lantern with one of the wooden matches she kept to open stubborn, clogged paint tubes. She selected a long-handled shovel from the stack of tools, and dragging it behind her, went into the garden.

The bush could be lifted out later, as Nellie had directed. Now time was the important element, for she had to have positive proof that the figurines were in the garden before anyone stopped her. And she had to work carefully. Most likely the Queens had been buried in some kind of container, but in case they were not, she couldn't run the risk of chipping them.

Gingerly she sank the shovel into the earth in front of the Vitex, at the spot Mike had indicated he had seen the man planting the bulbs. As Drake predicted, the ground was heavy. She did not attempt to turn over the soil, merely probed at intervals of every few inches hoping to strike something unyielding, then she'd start digging in earnest.

Behind her, Connie heard footsteps on the gravel path and a familiar half-cough, half-laugh. "Miss Blair."

Tightening her grip on the shovel, Connie turned and raised it defensively. Drake, wearing his overcoat and hat, was coming toward her. He stopped almost in front of her.

"Why, Miss Blair!"

In the light from the lantern she was relieved to see that the expression on his pudgy face was anything but menacing. Lowering the shovel, she said sheepishly, "Oh, I thought—"

"I only wanted to say good-by," he remarked formally, but pleasantly, recovering quickly from his surprise. "I hope you have enjoyed your association with the Calder Insurance Company despite my occasional . . . er . . . abruptness and your unfortunate experience of being locked in the cellar by mistake."

"Oh, I didn't mind too much," Connie replied,

trying to conceal her astonishment at his unexpected attitude. "Anyhow, Mr. Butterfield apologized."

Drake looked blank. "Apologized? I don't understand. How could he apologize when he didn't know he'd done it? Or did you tell him"—a slight edginess crept into his voice—"after you promised not to?"

"No. Didn't you?"

"No-o. Well"—Drake shrugged—"it's of little importance. And now I must be getting home. Good night, Miss Blair."

Connie watched him walk off across the garden and disappear into the shadows of the alley beyond. So it had been no mistake! Butterfield had known she was in the cellar and had locked her in on purpose. His mistake had been in apologizing.

Slowly, as on a television screen, the picture of the mystery that had been dissolving and superimposing suddenly came into sharp focus in her mind.

For a moment, Connie panicked. Could her scream be heard above the noise of homeward-bound traffic? Should she rush after Mr. Drake?

She eyed the house apprehensively. The last light had been turned off and it was in complete darkness. Wheeling about, Connie began to ram the shovel furiously. She couldn't run away now —she had a mission to perform. She *had* to find the Queens, for as long as they remained hidden, anyone alone in the Calder mansion was in grave peril.

CHAPTER 15

The Queens Are Found

THERE were three feet or more of the bed to be covered where the spurious tulip-bulb planter had worked. The probing had to be done—and fast! If the shovel chipped one of the Queens, it was just too bad, there was no time now to be careful. She *had* to locate them before anything happened to stop her search. She *had* to have proof of their presence, tangible evidence that would show Mr. Calder she had been correct— that the figurines had been stolen and this was a case for immediate police action.

Her fright of a few minutes ago was gone now, forgotten in the urgency of the moment as she plunged the shovel again and again into the ground.

At last it hit something hard and Connie's

heart skipped a beat. Was it a rock . . . or . . .
She edged the shovel farther down, pushed forward, and felt it slide across a flat surface. Straining, she lifted a spadeful of the moist dirt, then another and another, until she had dug about a foot deep. Dropping the shovel, she moved the lantern closer to her, fell to her knees and plunged her arms into the hole, scratching out the loose earth at the bottom with her cupped hands.

It was a box, she realized with elation, the top of a wooden box. She bent her head farther forward, trying to see it more closely.

Suddenly her whole body stiffened. She was no longer alone in the garden. Just behind her she heard heavy breathing. Before she could look up, the lantern was extinguished.

She started to scream, but a pair of hands, one clamped over her mouth and the other at the back of her neck, smothered her voice and the scream died, no louder than a wheeze.

Struggling to her feet, she frantically fought to free herself from the rigid grip of the man behind her. And then, in her mind's eye, she saw the familiar face of her attacker. She groped for her assailant's head, grabbed a large wad of thick hair in her fingers, and yanked hard.

She was released so abruptly that she toppled over on her side. As she righted herself, she knew the hair pulling had not caused her freedom. The whole garden was alive with the sound of running feet and familiar voices.

She recognized Lance's when he shouted: "Get him, Mike! He's headed your way!"

She knew Happy's when he called, as she heard him racing toward her: "Connie, are you hurt?"

"No . . . but . . . but—" She didn't finish. Instead, she scrambled to her feet and stood listening to the loud noise of scuffling on the gravel path at the other end of the garden. The noise lasted for only a second and ended in a triumphant cry:

"I got bracelets on 'im, but begorra can he fight!"

Happy came up to her and, without a word, threw his arms around her. Looking over his shoulder, Connie saw the rear door of the house open. The oblong of welcome light from the hall spilled out on the porch and beyond to the two figures on the path, reflecting on Mike's silver badge and Butterfield's familiar, gray hair.

Simultaneously, she heard Mike exclaim to his chained captive, "Well, if it ain't you—the little bulb planter!"

Then, Mr. Calder, framed in the doorway, demanded loudly, "What's going on here? Someone catch the prowler?"

Connie rested her head on Happy's shoulder. For a moment, she was afraid she was about to cry. "Hap," she asked, "how did you get here?"

Happy patted the back of her hair. "Lance came out to the campus late this afternoon and got me. He was plenty worried—said he knew

Frantically she fought to free herself

you'd discovered something during your conversation with Nellie, and he had your bush deal pretty well sized up. Incidentally, Connie, if you and Lance ever form a company and go into competition with the Pinkerton Agency, you'll have a good chance of success. But don't do it while I'm around—I get too shook up!"

A match flared beside them and Happy took his arms away. Connie hadn't noticed Lance's approach through the dark garden, but he was stooping, relighting the lantern. "Won't Montgomery ever learn?" he mumbled.

"I think he will now, Lance." Connie smiled, pointing to the hole in the flower bed. "Look! The Queens!"

"Good girl, Connie. You okay?"

"Will someone please tell me what this is all about?" Mr. Calder asked, coming into the circle of light, followed by Mike with the handcuffed Mr. Butterfield.

"I will, Montgomery," Lance offered. "Just before Aunt Carrie died, to my astonishment I got a letter from her, complete with a key to the old kitchen, telling me she'd had the Queens secretly hidden on the smoke shelf. She didn't say who she'd had put them there. My instructions were to keep an eye on them and make sure Maryanne got them. I did keep my eye on them, but about three days before Maryanne's boat docked, they disappeared."

"Lance!" Mr. Calder exclaimed. "Why didn't you tell me that then?"

"Well, I wasn't too worried at first. You'd told me yourself, Mont, about demolishing the out-building, so I figured they'd been removed for safety's sake—figured maybe whoever had hidden them had the same instructions I had. Old Carrie did queer things, you know—"

"That wasn't queer," Connie interrupted. "That was smart. When it finally dawned on me, here in the garden after Mr. Drake left, that no provident woman would have left such a confidence to one individual, I had an insight into your role in the mystery, Lance. I knew, then, you'd been hunting the stolen Queens, the same as I was."

Lance laughed. "And you were a real thorn in my side, Connie. I was scared green you'd find the Queens and not the culprit. And that was the last thing I wanted to happen. I'm sorry I had to use that ruse about your aunt being sick yesterday, but I was sure Butterfield would make a try for them and I didn't want you to mess up my chance of catching him. It was the only thing I could think of at the moment."

Lance didn't enlarge, but, remembering Mary-anne's description of his school days—when anything was missing—Connie understood. Because of his father's unfortunate mistake, Lance had been afraid the family would think he had stolen the figurines.

"Let's get to the bottom of this quickly," Mr. Calder insisted. "How did Butterfield come to be mixed up in it?"

"I'm not sure *how*," Lance said, frowning. "But I always knew he *was*."

"I know how," Connie spoke up brightly. "His first name probably is Andrew—the one who was mentioned in the obituary notice I found in the cellar—and he's the son of an old beau of Miss Calder. He lives nearby and when Miss Calder wanted the Queens hidden, she thought of him. I doubt if she'd even met him. More than likely, she called him on an impulse. Am I right, Mr. Butterfield?"

Everyone turned toward Butterfield, and when he made no reply, Mike announced, "Tell you what, I'll take him along down to the precinct, book him, and get a confession. That'll clear up the whole story for you."

Connie watched Mike walk his captive off across the garden toward the gate. She felt almost sorry for Butterfield. He hadn't any of the outward characteristics of a criminal. Possibly he had gotten himself into a situation he hadn't bargained for. "Lance," she queried, "what made you suspect Butterfield?"

"Show her the photograph, Lance," Happy directed, "the one you showed me this afternoon —the one with Handy-Andy Andrew and the underworld char—"

"*Daddy!*" The call carried across the garden. "Daddy, what are you doing?"

"Oh, good heavens, I forgot the twins!" Mr. Calder exclaimed. "I left them parked in the car while I came into the house to get the bush."

Edie and Enid came running along the path. "Why, there's Miss Blair," they cried in unison when they came abreast of the group gathered around the lantern.

"I bet she's found the little statues," Enid said to her sister.

"Sure she has." Edie pointed to the flower bed. "See—they're buried in that hole. Remember, Enid, I told you they must be buried. People always bury treasure."

Oh, for the mind of a child, Connie thought. If she had worked on the premise of buried treasure, she might have solved the mystery long ago. Aloud she said:

"I'm sure the little statues are in that hole, girls, and I think it's time we dug them up." Again she was consumed with a desire to see them. The facts of the mystery could wait. "I only wish your cousin Mrs. Jessup were here to open the box. After all, they're rightfully hers."

"She's here, all right," the twins replied in their usual chorus. "She's outside in the car. She sent us into the house to find out what was keeping Daddy."

"You see," Enid explained, "Cousin Maryanne took the train to town to avoid the awful traffic. She helped us buy a Christmas present for Mother and she's coming home with us for dinner. Then Daddy'll drive her to her place."

"It's only a few miles," Edie finished.

"Girls, go get Maryanne," Mr. Calder ordered patiently. "Obviously I have a weak mind"—he smiled as the twins trotted off jubilantly through the house—"as evidenced by my attitude about this whole affair. But I have the strong back that goes with it. If one of you boys will give me a hand, we'll get this box out of the ground. There are more shovels in the supply room."

"I'll get them," Happy offered. "In the meantime, Lance, show Connie that photograph."

Lance reached into his coat pocket and handed Connie a print. By the light of the lantern she saw that it was a picture of two men standing in front of a store. The sign read: *Antiques.* The man facing the camera, evidently the dealer, Connie mentally catalogued as a "plug-ugly." The man with his back to the camera was Butterfield; the hair showing white on the print, and the familiar old sweater, were unmistakable.

"I was taking some shots of store fronts on Pine Street for a real-estate broker just before Mont wangled me the job with Reid and Renshaw for the Sansom account," Lance told her. "When I came here to work, Butterfield seemed familiar. I went home, got out this negative and printed it and, sure enough, there he was!

"Now it wasn't inconceivable that Butterfield had a dealer friend on Pine Street," Lance went on, "but notice the expression on the dealer's face?"

Connie nodded. "As belligerence goes, I'd say it was the *most!*"

"Exactly. And a mere friend doesn't look that way at another friend. Butterfield had made this gent mad—and why? Take it from there, Connie," Lance finished.

Connie thought for a minute and then came up with an answer. "Mr. B had sold this man something he couldn't deliver. He'd sold him the figurines he'd buried and they were frozen solid in the ground. He needed time to get them out with a pick and shovel—and with Mike hovering around, and the watchman, and all the activity going on at the house, he didn't have a chance."

She looked at the photograph again. "Was the plug-ugly in the picture the 'underworld character' Happy encountered entering the house yesterday?" she asked.

"Yes, Happy recognized his picture right off. And that's why we were so worried about you, Connie. I did some investigating on him and he's nobody to trifle with. He had Butterfield over a barrel—he wanted the Queens and he wouldn't stop at anything. It's a wonder none of us got done in, including the watchman."

Mr. Calder, who had been listening intently to the conversation, cleared his throat. "This talk is very upsetting. I think the safest plan is to get these things out of their hiding place at once, as soon as Happy brings the shovels. There are half a dozen figurines, aren't there, Lance?"

"Five," Lance corrected.

"Five?" Connie repeated, astonished. "I thought there were six."

"There were six. But we'll find only five in the box."

CHAPTER 16

Happy Christmas

"Why, Lance," Connie queried, "how do you know that one figurine will be missing from the box?"

"Because I caught a glimpse of it standing on the bench in the supply room on Saturday night. I presume Butterfield kept it out for bargaining purposes—a sample of the buried contemporaries. He undoubtedly intended digging up the others Saturday night and delivering them *en masse* to Mr. Plug-Ugly. But before he got to it, he became suspicious that someone was spying on him from the garden—which, of course, I was. As he switched off his flash and came out to investigate, I saw him jam the statuette into the pocket of his coveralls."

Lance paused for breath. In the lantern light the fine bone structure of his lean face was emphasized to a degree that made him almost handsome.

"I thought for sure I had him trapped with the red-hot goods"—Lance smiled, and Connie was aware of the strong family resemblance between him and Mr. Calder—"but when Happy made all that clatter with the cat food, Butterfield scooted out the gate. Then we started our runaround. I chased Butterfield, Happy chased me—and you, Hap told me, ended in the graveyard! You see, Connie, I didn't know about that until this afternoon. After Butterfield gave me the slip in the cemetery I ran toward the river. He, apparently, headed uptown."

"And I"—Connie laughed—"was Impedimenta Number One. He had to get by me without my seeing him, so over the wall I went."

Lance nodded. "That sums it up. He had to shake us all with that Queen in his possession. I wonder what he did with it?" Lance mused.

Happy's arrival with the shovels stopped further conversation. Immediately Mr. Calder, Lance, and Happy peeled off their overcoats and got ready for work.

"I'll take them inside with me," Connie offered, gathering the coats in her arms. "And I think you're getting at the Queens just in time. This spell of moderate weather seems about over." It was getting colder by the minute. The bite she had felt in the air last night was even more intense now. Tomorrow threatened to be below freezing again.

"Connie!" Maryanne cried as she and the twins burst into the hall while Connie was stowing the coats on the bench. "Connie, the girls have just told me. *You've found the Queens!*"

"Only five, Mrs. Jessup," Connie conceded, suddenly realizing, in amusement, that the twins must have told a babblingly involved story to have kept them so long in returning. "However, I suppose you want to know about everything."

Maryanne did. Together, with the twins, they sat on the stairs. Connie reviewed the events of the last three days, touching only lightly on her own personal dangers. Before she had quite finished the narrative, the men appeared, carrying a long box that once had contained a shipment of ax handles.

"There's your precious inheritance," Mr. Calder announced as they placed the box in the center of the living-room floor. "Open it, Maryanne. Miss Blair says you're the one to do it." Kneeling, he pried up the nails that held the lid. "Now, don't be upset if you don't see the little statues right off," he cautioned the twins. "They're probably wrapped in something."

Maryanne lifted the loosened lid. At first glance the entire box seemed to be filled with hair-felt insulation.

"That stuff comes in rolls. Just pull off the top, Mrs. Jessup," Happy directed.

In fuzzy handfuls, Maryanne pulled off the hair felt and piled it on the floor. Under the insulating material was a covering of heavy oiled paper, under the oiled paper a layer of absorbent cotton.

Gingerly Maryanne rolled back the cotton.

For a full minute no one in the group encircling the box spoke. The five Queens were lying side by side, face up, breath-takingly beautiful. The chiseled features, the delicate coloring, the detail of their clothes was unbelievably exquisite, but it was in their crowns that the artist had reached the highest perfection of his skill. Set into the porcelain, the tiny headdress of each royal lady was constructed of a myriad of diminutive stones—faceted rubies that glowed with the warm fire of live coals. No wonder Earle Filmore had said that the hue was one that could never again be reproduced.

Edie broke the silence. "Which one isn't there?" she asked.

"Boadicea, Queen of the Britons," Maryanne told her. "But it doesn't matter. I'm so happy to have—"

"There's the 'phone," Lance said. "You answer it, Connie. If it's the police, you deserve to be first to hear whatever gives."

To Connie's delight, it was Mike on the other end of the line.

Butterfield had made a full confession. As Mike recounted it, Connie realized that she and Lance, working separately, had constructed the situation quite accurately. Butterfield had received a note from Miss Calder, whom he had never met, telling him that she and his father once had been sweethearts, and asking him to do her a favor because of the old friendship.

She had explained that she wanted the figurines hidden, but that if she asked any of the family to do it, they would have had a million-and-one other suggestions, including putting them in a bank vault, which she considered a silly expense for the brief months her niece would be in Europe.

Butterfield agreed to hide them for her, and his instructions, in the case of her death, tallied with the directions Miss Calder had given Lance. Butterfield honestly intended to see that Maryanne got them, but his greatest fault was gambling, and just before Maryanne returned he was hopelessly in debt.

Not knowing that anyone else knew the whereabouts of the Queens, he decided to sell them, and because he was afraid to risk keeping them all in his cheap rooming house, he buried five of them. With the sixth, he contacted an unscrupulous dealer and talked him into a sizable sum of advance money. Unfortunately for Butterfield, the dealer turned out to be not only unscrupulous, but an underworld character, a notorious "fence," an outlet for marketing stolen goods. He kept hounding Butterfield for the treasure. His unexpected appearance on Fifth Street the first night Connie was in the cellar, explained why Butterfield had locked her in . . .

"As much for your safety," Mike said, "as anything else. Butterfield didn't know what was going to happen, but the man only wanted to be shown the exact spot where the Queens were hidden. He was going to let you out again, but just when he got rid of the man, Mr. Drake released you."

After Butterfield realized that Connie had been searching the cellar, he tore off the obituary notice containing his father's name, which Miss Calder had told him was in the basement, in case it might prove significant. He wanted Connie to know, Mike went on, that he had never meant her harm. He had pushed her over the wall in desperation. And in the garden, tonight, the only thing he had in mind was to tie her up until he could get the Queens, deliver them, and make a getaway. Except for the revelation as to where Boadicea was, the rest of Butterfield's confession was familiar to Connie. She thanked Mike for calling and went back to the living room.

"Boadicea is waiting at the police station to be picked up," she announced. "She's been living under an old shirt in Mr. Butterfield's bureau drawer." And then Connie told them of her talk with Mike.

"Well," Mr. Calder exclaimed when she had finished, "that's quite a tale! But why would Aunt Carrie have entrusted the Queens to Butterfield? I mean, he *is* a character—"

"She probably didn't realize that, Mont," Lance chimed in. "Undoubtedly he got all dolled up for his visit with her and looked quite respectable. Also, if she interrogated him about his business, he may have told her that he worked for the Restoration. And with his background and education, Aunt Carrie most likely thought he had a job of some consequence and was impressed."

Happy laughed. "You're right, Lance. I heard him tell someone over the 'phone once that he worked for the Restoration. And, in effect, he did. He'd been with the construction company for years, I understand, and they've done most of the rebuilding around here."

"But the address of his rooming house," Mr. Calder mused. "Wouldn't that have conveyed anything to her?"

Lance shook his head. "No. That street is a conglomeration—run-down places alongside houses restored to very attractive town residences. Unless Aunt Carrie had gone to check— which she wouldn't have done since she rarely went out—she'd have no way of knowing in which he lived."

"Well," Mr. Calder said, grinning, "all that to the contrary, I can't get over Aunt Carrie's having a beau!"

"Nor I," Maryanne added.

"But remember, Maryanne," Enid interposed, "Great-Aunt Carrie was date age in the olden days."

Maryanne smiled. "Well, I wouldn't say 'olden days' exactly, Enid, but you're partly right. I guess your father and I weren't born."

Mr. Calder glanced at his watch. "Great Scott,

it's after seven. If we're late for dinner again, the cook will quit. Gather up your dolls, Maryanne. We'll collect Boa—whatever her name is on the way home."

"Let me carry one," Edie implored.

"And me," Enid said.

Cautioning them to be very careful, Maryanne handed each of the girls a figurine and turned to Connie. "Connie dear, isn't there something I can do to show you my appreciation? Some—" She hesitated and Connie realized she was fumbling for the right word rather than the mention of a reward.

"Well," Connie deliberated, "since it was the twins' dead rabbit that made me think the Queens were buried—and since the S.P.C.A. is having a drive for funds for a new building—"

Maryanne didn't let her finish. "Connie, those animals will have running water in every room." She laughed, highly pleased with the intimated suggestion. "I will donate to the building fund in your name."

"Come on, Lance, get your coat on," Mr. Calder said, starting for the door. "I'll drop you off."

When the others had gone, Happy turned to Connie and said, "And I'll drop *you*. The convertible is straddling the alley and its owner doesn't know where it is. I grabbed the keys from his dresser, so Lance and I could get going on our rescue mission. Before my roommate sends out an alert for a stolen car . . ."

Connie tried to smooth her disheveled hair as

Happy pulled out of the alley. "You know, Connie," he said, turning the car into Fifth Street, "if I'd realized that 'Handy Andy' wasn't just something the workmen called Butterfield because of his job—if it had dawned on me that his name really was Andrew—I might have connected him with Mr. Plug-Ugly instead of poor old Drake."

"Poor Mr. Drake," Connie sighed. "He turned out quite nice, and I condemned him from the start. I feel awful about that."

"We all make mistakes," Happy comforted her. "Say, look," he said brightly, pointing to a sign ahead of them. "Only thirteen shopping days 'til Christmas. Feature that, and me with not a present bought."

"Happy, are you going to Florida to be with your family for Christmas?" Connie asked.

"No. No wheels and no wings of my own— and the public transportation is too expensive. I'm staying in town."

"Well, if you don't mind rooming with my kid brother, three white mice, a chameleon, a bowl of tropical fish, and a parakeet, would you like to come to Meadowbrook?"

"Golly, Connie, I'd sure like to. But there's one thing that bothers me, though."

"What's that?"

"Your twin sister. I'm not sure how I'll act with two beautiful blondes around."

"Oh, Hap, it's going to be a wonderful 'Happy Christmas!' "